The Flowers of War

GELING YAN

Translated from the Chinese
by Nicky Harman

OTHER PRESS NEW YORK

Other Press edition 2012

Copyright © 2006 by Geling Yan

First published with the title *Jingling Shisan Chai* in 2006
English translation copyright © 2012 by Nicky Harman
English translation first published in Great Britain
in 2012 by Harvill Secker

This publication was assisted by a grant from
China Book International.

Special thanks from Other Press to Rebecca Carter of
Harvill Secker for her dedication, promptness, and generosity.

Production Editor: Yvonne E. Cárdenas
Design revisions for this edition by Cassandra J. Pappas

10 9 8 7 6 5 4 3 2 1

Library of Congress Cataloging-in-Publication Data

Yan, Geling.
    [Jin ling shi san chai. English]
    The flowers of war / Geling Yan ; translated from the Chinese by Nicky Harman.
        p. cm.
    Summary: "December 1937. The Japanese have taken Nanking. A group of terrified schoolgirls hides in the compound of an American church. Among them is Shujuan, through whose thirteen-year-old eyes we witness the shocking events that follow. Run by the Father Engelmann, an American priest who has been in China for many years, the church is supposedly neutral ground in the war between China and Japan. But it becomes clear the Japanese are not obeying international rules of engagement. As they pour through the streets of Nanking, raping and pillaging the civilian population, the girls are in increasing danger. And their safety is further compromised when prostitutes from the nearby brothel climb over the wall into the compound seeking refuge. Short, powerful, vivid, this beautiful novel transports the reader to 1930s China. Full of wonderful characters, from the austere priest to the irreverent prostitutes, it is a story about how war upsets all prejudices and how love can flourish amidst death"—Provided by publisher.
    ISBN 978-1-59051-556-3 (pbk.) — ISBN 978-1-59051-557-0 (ebook)
    I. Harman, Nicky. II. Title.
    PL2925.K55J5613 2012
895.1'352—dc23   2011047424

To my father, Xiao Ma

The Flowers of War

One

Shujuan woke with a start. The next thing she knew, she was standing beside her bed. It was about five in the morning, a little earlier perhaps. At first she thought it was the absence of gunfire that had woken her. The artillery that had been thundering for days had suddenly fallen silent. Then she noticed a warm stain on her cotton nightgown. She stood barefoot and dazed. Blood. The wetness quickly turned icy cold. So, it had finally happened to her, as it does to every woman.

Her makeshift bed was in a row of eight. There was a narrow gangway and then another eight beds. Buildings all over Nanking were burning and light from the flames filtered through the blackout curtains that covered the small oval attic windows. Orange patterns rippled across the room. Shujuan could make out the sleeping forms of the other girls and hear their deep breathing as they dreamed of more peaceful days.

She pulled a jacket over her shoulders and climbed down through the trapdoor in the floor to the workshop below. The workshop was used for printing and binding the pamphlets and hymn sheets that the St Mary Magdalene mission needed for church services and its other religious work. Usually the attic above was unoccupied. The trapdoor was merely to allow access for electrical or roof repairs. It was connected to a ladder by an ingenious mechanism that extended the ladder downwards as soon as the cover was opened.

When Shujuan and fifteen classmates had arrived at the mission compound the previous evening, Father Engelmann had told them to stay upstairs in the attic as much as possible. They had been given a tin bucket to urinate in. But the blood on her nightdress was an emergency. Shujuan needed to go to the washroom.

Father Engelmann hadn't expected that he would have to give the St Mary Magdalene schoolgirls shelter. Yesterday afternoon he, Deacon Adornato and their two servants, Ah Gu and George Chen, had taken those pupils who had been unable to leave school down to the river to get the ferry to Pukou. But they had been unable to board. When the steamer pulled into the dock, a group of badly wounded soldiers appeared and pushed the girls aside. One of the soldiers told Father Engelmann that their division had been shot at, not by the Japanese, but by their own side. They had received orders to make an emergency retreat but had clashed with Chinese soldiers who had not received the same order and so thought they were deserters. Having obeyed instructions to destroy their heavy weaponry on leaving the battlefield, they were a sitting target. They were machine-gunned and came under artillery fire, and some were then crushed by tanks. Losses and injuries on the retreating side ran into the hundreds before the misunderstanding was sorted out. No doubt out of a sense of guilt, the unit who had inflicted the injuries took over the boat at gunpoint, and put the wounded onboard. There was no room for the clergymen and the girls.

Father Engelmann had felt that it was too dangerous to stay by the river. He and Deacon Adornato had led their little party back through the alleyways of Nanking to the church, with Ah Gu and George Chen bringing up the rear.

Shujuan clambered down the wooden ladder that creaked at each step she made. On reaching the floor of the workshop, she felt the bone-chilling December damp seep through the soles of her slippers. Standing on one of the tables near the ladder was a thick candle melted into a shapeless mass of wax. Its quivering sprout of light gave Shujuan a little comfort as she felt her way across the workshop. Father Engelmann had promised the girls that, when daylight came, they would return to the dock and, if there was no ferry, they would make for the Safety Zone and take refuge there instead.

As Shujuan groped her way down the corridor made by the work tables, the candle went out like a sigh. She stopped, disoriented. The silence frightened her. Over the past days, she and her schoolmates had become accustomed to the thunder of artillery and machine guns. The lack of gunfire was disquieting. Not peaceful but ominous, as if Nanking were surrendering. But how could that be? Only a day ago Father Engelmann had reassured them that the city was impregnable. The sturdy city walls and the Yangtze River meant that it would be extremely difficult for the Japanese to take the city.

Almost all the pupils who had been left at the school were

orphans. Only Shujuan and Xiaoyu had parents, but they were abroad and had waited until too late to come and fetch their daughters. Shujuan felt utterly betrayed. Clearly her cowardly parents had not wanted to come back to a capital city abandoned even by the Chinese government.

In the washroom, she stood by the toilet and examined her nightdress. She was torn between curiosity and disgust at the dark liquid issuing from deep within her belly. She had the sense that this blood had turned her flesh into fertile soil, a place where any demon could implant a seed which would put forth shoots and bear fruit. Shuddering, she wedged a bulky cloth into her underwear and left the washroom, walking in an ungainly fashion. In the workshop she went to the window and pulled aside the blackout curtains. The bell tower of the Gothic church loomed in the night. It had been shelled a few days before and, along with the main entrance to the compound, had been reduced to rubble. The only way into the compound now was by a smaller side door. Behind the church she could just make out the lawn. Father Engelmann was passionate about this patch of grass. It was, he said proudly to his congregation, the last island of green left in Nanking. For decades it had served as a place for holding charity sales and celebrating weddings and funerals. Now it was dominated by the two flags – the Stars and Stripes and a Red Cross one – that lay on the grass as a signal to aircraft that it was neutral territory. In spring and summer, the lushness of the grass formed a fairy-tale setting for Father Engelmann's red-brick rectory.

Shujuan stared up at the ruined tower which, silhouetted against the fires that raged outside, still retained some of its grandeur. There was a glimmer of dawn in the east. It looked as if it would be a beautiful day. Climbing back up the ladder, she slipped quietly into bed and fell into a deep sleep.

*   *   *

Shujuan was woken not long afterwards by shrieks and wails coming from downstairs. Together with the other girls she jumped out of bed and ran over to the windows. Pushing aside the blackout curtains and tearing away the rice paper from the window frames, they managed to get a view of the front courtyard.

Shujuan pressed the side of her face up against the window frame. She saw Father Engelmann run out from behind the church, his ample cassock flapping like a sail. 'You're not allowed over the wall!' he was shouting. 'We've got no food!'

Some of the bolder pupils opened a window. Now they could take it in turns to stick their heads out and see better. Sitting on top of the wall, above the side door, were two young women. One was wearing a bright pink satin dressing gown which made her look like a newly wedded wife who had just jumped out of bed. The other wore a fox-fur stole over a tight cheongsam.

Fascinated by the drama, the girls climbed, one by one, down the ladder, walked through the workshop and went to huddle together in the doorway. By the time Shujuan arrived, there were another four women on top of the wall. Despite Father Engelmann's attempts to keep them out, the first two had succeeded in jumping down. By this time Ah Gu and George Chen had joined the fray.

Father Engelmann noticed the chattering girls and yelled fiercely, 'Ah Gu! Take those girls away. They mustn't see these women!'

He looked tired. He hadn't been able to shave since the water had been cut off, and the growth of stubble on his face made him look older than his sixty years.

'They're from the brothels!' exclaimed some of the more sophisticated girls.

'What brothels?'

'The Qin Huai River brothels!'

Deacon Fabio Adornato came hurrying out of the church building, shouting at the women: 'Get out! We're not taking in refugees!' There was a momentary lull in the weeping and wailing as the women stared in astonishment at the big-nosed foreigner who spoke in authentic, unadulterated Yangzhou dialect, the kind spoken by cooks and barbers. But it didn't last for long.

'We ran away from the river but our cart overturned and the horse bolted,' cried one of the women. 'The city's full of Jap soldiers and we can't get into the Safety Zone!'

'There's no room to swing a cat in the Safety Zone, it's crammed!' chimed in a younger girl.

'I know someone in the US embassy,' shouted another, her words tumbling over each other. 'He offered to hide us there, but last night he went back on his word. He just turned us away! All that fun we gave him – all for nothing!'

'Fucker!' said someone else casually. 'When they come looking for pleasure, it's all "Sweetheart this" and "Sweetheart that", but then . . . !'

Shujuan was flabbergasted at their language. She had never heard anything like it. Ah Gu tried to pull her away but she resisted. George, the cook, under orders to use a

8

stout stick on the women to keep them out, was flailing to left and right of him, begging them: 'Please, girls, go! You'll only die of hunger or thirst if you come in here! The students only get two bowls of gruel a day and there's no running water. That's enough now, off you go!' Shujuan noticed that he was half-hearted in the way he brandished his stick. It hit the brick walls, the ground, but never the women. In fact, the only person who got hurt was himself as the blows jarred his fingers and wrists.

Suddenly one of the women knelt down in front of Father Engelmann and bowed her head. All Shujuan could see was her back, but it was an unforgettable back, as lithe and expressive as a face might be. Father Engelmann was trying to argue with the woman in the Chinese that he had learned so painstakingly over the last thirty years. He was reiterating what George had said: there was no food, no water, and no room. Hiding more people endangered everyone. When it was clear he was not getting his message across, he said in frustration, 'Fabio, translate for me!'

Deacon Fabio Adornato was born to Italian-American parents but brought up in a village in Yangzhou. He spoke in such perfect Yangzhou dialect that people called him 'Yangzhou Fabio'.

The woman knelt as if she had taken root, but her shoulders and back were alive with meaning.

'Our lives are worthless,' she said, 'not worth rescuing. All we're asking for is a good death. Even the lowliest of beasts, pigs and dogs, deserve a clean, merciful death.'

There was no denying her elegance and dignity. As she spoke, her chignon suddenly came undone and hair cascaded down over her shoulders. It was beautiful hair.

Father Englemann explained in his broken Chinese that among the pupils in his care there were some from the highest echelons of society, whose parents were long-standing members of his congregation. In the last few days they had cabled asking him to keep their daughters from harm. He had answered each cable swearing that he would guard them with his life.

Fabio lost patience. 'You're wasting your breath talking like this to them. There's only one sort of language they understand: George, start being a proper Monkey King and give them a real beating!'

Ah Gu had given up trying to take Shujuan indoors and now rushed out and made a grab for George's stick. Then one of the women suddenly fainted. As she fell into Ah Gu's arms, her mangy mink coat slid open to reveal a white, naked body. Ah Gu let out a cry. The women on the wall took advantage of the diversion to hop nimbly down into the courtyard. A stout, dark-skinned woman stayed on top of the wall to hoist up an assortment of others, all of whom were unmistakably prostitutes.

Fabio was in despair. 'That's enough!' he shouted. 'We've got every single whore from the Qin Huai brothels here!' Meanwhile Ah Gu was trying to extricate himself from the embrace of the woman who had fainted but she hung on like a limpet, and the more he struggled, the more she tightened her hold.

Father Engelmann, unable to stop this gaudy tidal wave of females, was looking crestfallen. 'Open the door,' he finally ordered Ah Gu.

Shujuan watched in horror as a colourful assortment of women swept in, cluttering the neatly swept, stone-flagged courtyard with their belongings: baskets, bundles and satin bed quilts from which tumbled hair ribbons, silk stockings and other intimate articles. How could her parents have left her to witness such a vile scene? It could only be because they were selfish and loved her less than her sister. It had been a niggling doubt, but now she was sure of it. Her little sister was their favourite. Her father had been awarded a scholarship to pursue his studies in America, and immediately declared that only her sister would go since she had not yet started school. Shujuan could not have her schooling interrupted by a trip overseas. Her mother backed her father. A year would fly by, they comforted Shujuan, and the whole family would soon be together again. Shujuan seethed with resentment against her parents as she watched George struggling with the woman in his arms. By now the front of the mink coat was wide open revealing an expanse of flesh the colour of sour milk. Shujuan shrank back into the doorway, her face aflame. Then she turned and fled back up to the attic, to which the other girls had already retreated to watch events from the windows.

There was pandemonium in the courtyard as the women ran around in search of food, water and a place to relieve themselves. One told another to hold up an expensive-looking bottle-green velvet cape in front of her, saying apologetically to the 'foreign monks' that they had been on the run all night. She could not wait any longer, she said, and disappeared behind the cape as if taking a curtain call.

'Animals!' yelled Fabio in English.

'Please control yourself, Fabio,' Father Engelmann said quietly. Then he turned to the prostitutes, including the one who had emerged cheerfully from behind the velvet cape and stood holding up her trousers by their cord. 'Since you have come to stay here –' he chose his words carefully – 'I beg you, as the priest of this church, to behave yourselves with decency.'

'Father, listen . . . !' expostulated Fabio.

'You listen to me! Let them come in,' said Father Engelmann. 'At least for today. Once the Japanese have completed their occupation, they'll have responsibility for keeping the peace in the city. Then we can ask these women to leave. The Japanese people are well known to be law-abiding. I'm sure their troops will soon impose order on this chaos.'

'They won't be able to impose order in a day!'

'Well then, two days. In the meantime, they can camp in the cellar.'

Father Engelmann turned and walked back towards his house. He had announced his decision and there was no room for further discussion.

'Father, I don't agree!' Fabio shouted after him.

Father Engelmann stopped and turned round. As invincibly refined as ever, he said quietly: 'I know you don't agree, Fabio.' Then he continued on his way. What he had not said was even clearer: *Your disagreement is not of the slightest importance to me.* His refinement conferred unchallengeable superiority. Although Fabio's American parents had died when he was young and he had been cared for by a Chinese woman in the countryside of Yangzhou, he looked down on lower-class Chinese in the same way that the local dignitaries or militia did. But if they were several rungs below him in the social scale, then so was he to Father Engelmann who regarded him as inferior because of his rural upbringing.

At that moment, a young prostitute made for the door of the building that housed the workshop. She had seen the girls' heads at the attic windows and felt sure that it would be a good place to go. At least it would be warmer and more comfortable than outside. Fabio grabbed her from behind but she slipped out of his grasp like an eel. Fabio made another attempt, and this time got hold of the bundle she carried on her back. It was of coarse cloth, less slippery than her satin dressing gown, and he managed to get a purchase and pull her away from the doorway. But the bundle came undone and a sudden hailstorm of small bone mah-jong pieces rained down on the ground. They were fine-quality pieces – you could tell that from the clear, clinking noise they made as they fell.

The stout, dark-skinned woman shouted: 'If you lose one piece, Cardamom, I'll skin your arse alive!'

'There's nothing wrong with my arse, Jade!' Cardamom shouted back. 'I bet he'd like a bit of it too!'

The schoolgirls exchanged amazed glances. Fancy a woman as dark-skinned as that having a name like Jade! As for the girl called Cardamom, she seemed barely older than they were.

Fabio had let go of Cardamom but her words, together with the threat that she might be around to say more things like this, goaded him into grabbing her again and pushing her towards the exit.

'Out! Get out! Ah Gu! Open the door for her!' His winter-pale face shone, as if he might break out in a sweat at any moment.

'Ai-ya! Master, you're my fellow countryman!' cried Cardamom. She stumbled and her voice became shrill. 'I beg you, please don't! I won't do it again!'

She had the face of a child, but her body was well developed and she simply bounced back every time he pushed her. 'Please, master! Teach me good manners, I promise I'll be good. I'm only fifteen years old! Sister Yumo! Put in a good word for me!'

The woman with the beautiful back put her bags and valuables in a neat pile and walked over to Fabio and Cardamom who were still struggling. Suddenly Shujuan could see her face. She realised the woman had not a slack bone in her entire body. Every part of her could smile or complain, and was capable of a subtle sign language.

'How many times have I told you to wash your mouth out, Cardamom?' Yumo said with a smile. She placed herself between the two of them, and pushed Cardamom back towards Jade.

Meanwhile, Ah Gu was cheerfully leading the women down into the cellar under the kitchen. The prostitutes, wide-eyed with curiosity, commented on everything as they pranced along behind him.

Pressed up against the attic window Shujuan watched the women go, her hands massaging her belly to ease the pain.

Two

During prayers that morning, there was the sound of gunfire as if fighting had broken out again somewhere in the city, the salvos coming fast and furious. It lasted for about half an hour. Despite this, Fabio insisted on going to the Safety Zone to find out whether it might still be possible to take the ferry. He came back at midday bringing only bad news. The girls listened wide-eyed as he told Father Engelmann how the streets were lined with corpses, mostly civilians and including children and old people. According to the members of the International Commission in the Safety Zone, the Japanese were shooting anyone who did not understand commands bawled in Japanese, or who ran when they saw guns. They were using the bodies to fill in the holes gouged in the road surface by explosives. When Fabio had finished speaking, he forced a smile at the girls and then glanced back at Father Engelmann. The implication was that the Father had misjudged things. When there was carnage on this scale, how could order be restored within just a couple of days?

This was at lunch. The sixteen girls sat squeezed down both sides of the refectory table normally used by the clergymen. Since their arrival at the church, Father Engelmann had ordered George to serve him his twice-daily meals of porridge or noodle soup in his room. He was a firm believer that dignity was preserved by maintaining one's distance. He therefore put at least the patch of grass between himself and the schoolgirls. But as soon as he heard that Fabio was back from the Safety Zone, he had put down his bowl of porridge and hurried over.

'So food and water are critical, now that we've just taken in another fourteen women,' Fabio finished.

'How much food have we got left, George?' Father Engelmann asked.

'Two buckets of flour, fifty kilos or so,' said George, 'but only a peck of rice. There's no water but what's in the cistern . . . oh, and two barrels of wine.'

Fabio shot George a look. 'We can't possibly use wine to wash our faces or our clothes! You can't make tea with wine or cook food with it. Don't talk such rubbish!'

George did not like being patronised. *When the water gets low, you can drink wine instead, Deacon Adornato, since you drink it like water anyway!* he thought to himself.

'It's better than I imagined,' was Father Englemann's unexpected reaction.

'Fifty kilos of flour for so many people? We'll be living on air in a couple of days!' Fabio snapped at George. The cook was the only person he could vent his feelings on since he obviously had to speak civilly to Father Engelmann. George Chen, a twenty-year-old orphan with no family to protect him, was the frequent butt of other people's bad temper. George was a beggar Father Engelmann had rescued from the streets as a child and sent to cookery school. After a few months, he had come back to the church as a cook, and had changed his name to the English 'George'.

George ignored him and addressed Father Engelmann. 'There's a bit of rancid butter as well. You told me to throw it away, Father, but I hung on to it. And there's a jar of pickled vegetables. It's gone a bit mouldy and it doesn't smell so good, but it's fine to eat!' he announced triumphantly.

Father Engelmann seemed cheered by George's words. 'In a couple of days, things are bound to have settled down, believe me,' he said. 'I've been to Japan many times and they're the most courteous and friendly people in the world. The Japanese never permit a leaf out of place in a garden.'

The girls missed much of the substance of what Father Engelmann said, which they often did even though they had had English classes since they were small. But they were carried away by his infectious optimism and the exact words did not seem to matter.

Just after the priest had left, there was the sound of a commotion in the kitchen.

'What on earth . . . ?' exclaimed George and rushed off to investigate.

A moment later, a woman's voice asked: 'Has all the food gone?'

'There are still a few biscuits left,' Shujuan heard George say.

Instantly, the girls were on their feet and running in the direction of the voices. Shujuan got there first. George had betrayed them; he was selling off their meagre food supplies. They needed the biscuits to eat with their soup, which was so watery these days that on its own it did nothing to allay their hunger.

Three or four of the prostitutes were already tucking into the biscuits. Shujuan recognised their ringleader as Hongling, a curvaceous young woman whose volatile temper was easily aroused. When that happened, her slender eyebrows drew together to form two straight lines, indicating that it would be dangerous to cross her.

'George, how could you give away our biscuits to those women?' protested Shujuan, pronouncing the words 'those women' as if they were a term of abuse.

'But they came and took them!'

'They asked you and you handed them over!' Sophie exclaimed. Sophie was an orphan; her foreign name had been given to her by the mission schoolteachers.

'Ai-ya! Hoarding food, are we?' the dark-skinned prostitute called Jade said mockingly.

'Let us borrow just a bit, then tomorrow when the wonton sellers are out in the streets, we'll buy you dumplings in return, OK?' said Hongling.

'George, are you deaf?' yelled Shujuan, suddenly goaded to fury. First her parents had abandoned her like a stray dog to starve in this tumbledown church, now she was being betrayed by the cook and bullied by a whore . . .

'It was nothing to do with him. We found the biscuits ourselves,' said Hongling, her slender eyebrows arched like crescent moons.

'Was I talking to you?' Shujuan said, raising a hand threateningly at her smiling adversary.

Even her classmates were embarrassed at this. 'Leave her alone!' they muttered.

Hongling frowned. 'You little bitch! What you need is a good f—' But just at that moment a hand came round from behind her and stopped her mouth.

The hand belonged to Zhao Yumo. The row in the kitchen could clearly be heard in the cellar, and she had rushed up the ladder to put a stop to Hongling's foul language. It was evident to the girls that this prostitute was the leader of the pack.

*   *   *

Long after the prostitutes had gone back to their lair and her classmates to their attic, Shujuan sat despondently in the kitchen. Her outburst had left her drained, but her head still whirled with the exquisitely wounding insults she could have heaped on the women. She hated herself for not having taken the chance. She could hear the women chatting and teasing each other in the cellar below. They were obviously used to indulging in provocative banter with their male clients; they simply carried on in the same vein when there were no men around.

As she sat there in the gloom, Shujuan listened to the continuous rattle of gunfire. The damned Japs had fought their way into Nanking, cut her off from her grandparents, made her parents too afraid to come back to China, and let a bunch of whores invade Nanking's 'last island of green'. She was overwhelmed with anguish, and hatred for everything and everyone. She even began to hate herself, now it turned out she had the same body and organs as those women downstairs, and the same cramping pains expelling the same unclean blood from her body.

* * *

In the afternoon, Father Engelmann ventured out. George Chen drove him in the battered old Ford that Father Engelmann had had for years, and which of all his few worldly possessions was one of his most cherished. They only went a couple of kilometres towards the centre of the city before they turned back. This was a Nanking they did not recognise; a Nanking with its buildings demolished and streets strewn with corpses. George got lost several times. In a narrow street near the Zhonghua Gate, they came across Japanese troops escorting five or six hundred Chinese soldiers in the direction of Rain Flower Terrace which lay just outside the gate. Father Engelmann told George to stop the car, gathered his courage and enquired politely of the Japanese officer where they were taking their captives. An interpreter translated his question and the officer told him that they were being taken to clear some waste ground ready for cultivation.

When Father Engelmann arrived back at the church, he did not even touch his dinner but spent an hour sitting in the church. Then he called all the girls in and gave them a blunt description of what he had seen. He looked mildly at Fabio and admitted that his earlier judgement of the situation had been too optimistic. The biggest responsibility he now faced was to ensure that the thirty-odd people in his care did not starve before they found new supplies of food and water. He told George to search the compound from top to bottom, to see if anything had been missed, no matter if it was mouldy.

Before he had finished speaking, some of the prostitutes burst in through a side door. They stood in a huddle, curious to see what was going on in the church and whether it could be of any benefit to them. One look at the pupils' downcast faces told them there was nothing to be had and they turned to leave. But Fabio stopped them.

'Please keep to the cellar in future and don't come upstairs,' he said. 'Especially don't come here.'

'What do you mean by "here"?' asked one of the women flippantly.

'Wherever the schoolgirls are.'

Then Father Engelmann said suddenly, 'The Yong Jia soap factory must be on fire. The tallow they use to make soap must be burning, otherwise the fire wouldn't be so big.'

They followed his gaze. Through the open church door they could see that the early-evening darkness was ablaze. The fire lit up the surviving stained-glass windows of the church, making the bright colours of the Virgin and Child sparkle like jewels. The girls stared transfixed in terror at the magnificent sight. The flames illuminated the inside of the church with extraordinary clarity, throwing every surface and angle into sharp relief.

Ah Gu and George Chen agreed with Father Engelmann

that the fire must come from the Yong Jia soap factory in Outer Fifth Street. Fabio told the girls to go back up to the attic. Anything might happen this evening.

*   *   *

Later, as Fabio was walking towards the workshop building to check the trapdoor was closed, he was surprised to find the prostitute called Hongling in the doorway, a cigarette hanging from her lips.

'Where do you think you're going?' he asked sharply.

Hongling was peering intently at the ground. Startled, she dropped the cigarette, then bent down for it, sticking her ample buttocks in the air.

She giggled. 'Are you telling me I can't look for something I've lost?'

'Back to the cellar!' ordered Fabio, abruptly cutting her off. 'I'll kick you out if you don't obey the rules.'

'They call you Yangzhou Fabio, don't they?' she said, still with a smile on her face. 'Ah Gu's talked about you.'

'Did you hear what I said? Back to the cellar with you!' Fabio pointed in the direction of the kitchen.

'Help me look and then I'll go back. For a foreign

gentleman, you don't half sound like a Yangzhou peasant!'
She gave a laugh which made her quiver from head to toe.
'Anyway, you haven't asked me what I'm looking for,' she
said with a pout.

'What are you looking for?' he asked grudgingly.

'Mah-jong tiles. They fell out somewhere round here. Do
you remember where they went? When I picked them up
and counted them, there were five missing!'

'The nation's capital has fallen and you still want to play
mah-jong?'

'It didn't fall because we were playing,' she protested.
'Anyway, what else do you want us to do here? Die of
boredom?'

Fabio heard giggling above his head and looked up to see
the schoolgirls peering through the attic windows.

Aware that the girls were watching, Hongling immediately
started putting on even more of an act. She was no longer
the bedraggled figure she had been when she arrived. Her
hair was carefully combed and fastened with a turquoise satin
ribbon.

She shouted up to the girls: 'If you've got those five tiles,
you can't play, and we can't play without them.' The girls
looked at each other, and then one, bolder than the rest,

mimicked her Yangzhou accent back at her and they burst out laughing.

Fabio berated them: 'Whoever took her tiles, give them back!'

There was a chorus of voices from upstairs: 'Why would we want her tiles? We might catch nasty diseases from them!'

Hongling was furious. 'That's right!' she yelled back. 'I've got boils all over me, and the tiles were covered in the pus. Anyone who touches my tiles will catch my boils!'

The girls made hawking sounds and two of them spat through a window, just missing their target.

At that moment Zhao Yumo appeared, having discovered Hongling's absence.

'What the hell do you think you're doing?' she shouted. 'Give you an inch and you take a mile. Get back to the cellar!' Her shouts seemed to cost her some effort, as if disciplinary language like this did not come naturally to her.

Yumo frogmarched Hongling off towards the kitchen. As they walked past George, who was standing watching on the sidelines, Hongling pointed at Yumo and complained, 'We're in her clutches!' as if George could offer her protection.

Ignoring Fabio's injunctions to go to bed immediately,

the girls shouted belligerently at the retreating figures of the prostitutes: 'Come back! We'll give you the tiles!'

Hongling ran back. She craned her neck up at the attic windows, crammed with identical childish faces and reached out cupped hands. 'Give me them!'

Yumo could tell the girls were baiting Hongling and shouted at her: 'Have some pride, can't you!' But it was too late. Some bone tiles were hurled through the windows so hard they bounced on the ground. One of them hit Hongling on the cheek.

'Who did that?' Fabio yelled up at them. 'Xiaoyu! You were one of them!'

Hongling's face was red with anger. She wanted to climb the ladder to the attic and take her revenge.

'Forget it,' Yumo said. 'Let it go.'

'Why should I let it go?' Hongling protested.

Her accent – she was from a poor province north-west of Nanking – was very pronounced.

'Because these people have allowed us to stay in this rathole. Because they're prepared to put up with us. Because we've got no face to lose. Because when we're alive, we're less than human, and when we die, we're less than demons. Because we can be beaten and humiliated by anyone at will,' said Yumo.

Three

At night, the light from the fires was brighter than ever and the girls could not sleep. Xiaoyu had the bed next to Shujuan. Xiaoyu's father was one of the wealthiest men in the south, with businesses extending from Amoy to Hong Kong, Singapore and Japan. When a boycott of Japanese goods was introduced in Nanking, her father had changed the labels on all his Japanese goods and sold them as if they were manufactured in China. He did not lose a cent on the deal. He traded with Portuguese wine merchants and bought gallons of red and white wine at a bargain price or in exchange for raw silk. The red wine used by the church at Mass was also all supplied by him.

The relationship between Shujuan and Xiaoyu was fragile. Xiaoyu was pretty, and seemed not to understand that pretty girls could easily wound those who most admired them and longed to be their friends. Shujuan was just such a girl. The reason why Shujuan was easily hurt by Xiaoyu was that she was secretly unwilling to submit to her friend. Shujuan got top marks, and she was pretty too, but with Xiaoyu around, Shujuan could never shine. Between a pair like Xiaoyu and Shujuan, there was always an element of cruelty. And the one who was cruel and the one who was the victim of cruelty frequently swapped places.

Xiaoyu reached over to Shujuan to see if she was asleep. Shujuan felt it was beneath her dignity to respond straight away because yesterday Xiaoyu had been best friends with Sophie. Her lack of response seemed to make Xiaoyu more eager. She pressed harder with her arm and whispered in Shujuan's ear: 'Are you awake?'

'What's the matter?' asked Shujuan, pretending she had just woken up.

Xiaoyu leaned closer. 'Which do you think is the prettiest?' she said.

Shujuan was startled. She knew Xiaoyu was referring to the prostitutes, but she had not thought about any of them in this way. Still, she didn't want to disappoint Xiaoyu. Making up with her friend after a tiff was the sweetest feeling. 'Who do you think?' she said.

'Let's go and have another look,' said Xiaoyu.

The fact was that the prostitutes exerted a strange fascination over all the girls. Just thinking about the business they did with that secret place between their legs gave them a little spasm in their own bodies, which they concealed by blushing and exclaiming: 'Ai-ya!' There was nothing more seductive than sin and they took a vicarious delight in the fact that these women did bad things which they hardly dared contemplate.

Shujuan and Xiaoyu crept downstairs. The fires cast a lurid light over the church compound. An old American hickory tree with a magnificent canopy reared skyward as if somehow its bare branches were taking root in the golden night sky. An odd smell of burning reached their nostrils.

The two girls stood in the courtyard, forgetting why they had come down. It might just have been to check that Father Engelmann's red-brick rectory was still there. Or to see that the candle was still lit in the window of Fabio's bedroom next to the library. At that moment, however, the sound of music caught their attention. Someone was playing a tune on the *pipa*. The plucked strings made a beautiful sound.

They walked around behind the kitchen and came to the ventilation shafts that let air into the cellar. There were three of them, each one covered with a rusty iron grille. They made excellent spyholes.

It was Cardamom who was playing the *pipa*. She was an exquisitely pretty girl with an almond-shaped face. If you looked only at her eyes, she seemed to wear a constant smile. But her mouth had an aggrieved expression, as if she was constantly being short-changed. Nevertheless she was a beauty and could have bewitched anyone if she had not been a lowly prostitute. Looking down the spyhole, it did not take the two girls long to decide she was the prettiest of the women.

The cellar was not a cellar any more. It had been transformed into an underground brothel. The women had moved some books from the workshop down to the cellar, and had used them to form platforms on which to sleep. Those who had brought bedrolls had spread them over the cots: silk quilts in impossible pinks and greens, ready for a normal business day by the Qin Huai River. There were mirrors of various shapes standing on book stacks along the walls. The prostitute called Jade was plucking her eyebrows in front of a little heart-shaped mirror. The women's furs lay strewn around, and the hooks on which sausages and hams had once hung had been wrapped in the silver paper from cigarette packets and festooned with a garish assortment of scarves, wraps and brassieres.

Four women were standing round a wine barrel on which they had placed a large kitchen chopping board, and the girls could hear a pattering sound as they played mah-jong. The temporary loss of five tiles did not seem to have diminished their enthusiasm for the game. Each of the women had a bowl in front of her filled with red wine, presumably the wine used for Mass that was supplied by Xiaoyu's father.

'Nani! Let me play a round!' Cardamom said.

Nani pulled down the lower lid of her right eye with one lacquered fingernail. The girls standing above understood the gesture. 'In your dreams,' it meant. 'You can just watch.'

'Ai-ya! I'm so bored!' said Cardamom. She picked up Nani's bowl and took a swig of wine.

'Then go and ask the foreign monks for a couple of Bibles and read aloud to us,' Yumo teased her with a smile.

'I went up to the first floor in the foreign temple and

sneaked a look,' said Hongling. 'It's all books! Fabio's room is next to the library.'

'Us women could become Taoist nuns if we read all those Bibles,' said Hongling, and declared she had won the round.

She swept all her winnings into a pile in front of her.

'It wouldn't be such a bad thing to become a Taoist nun. You'd get fed,' said Jade.

'Well, you've got such a big belly to feed, it would be worth you becoming a nun,' said Nani.

'It would only be any fun if you hooked up with a foreign monk,' said Hongling with a giggle.

'They don't call them nuns in Taoist temples, do they, Yumo?' someone asked.

'It doesn't matter what they're called, they still have to be vegetarian and celibate,' said Yumo.

'Never mind the vegetarian food, you'd never get a good night's sleep if you had to be celibate, would you, Jade?'

There was a burst of laughter. Jade picked up a tile and aimed it at Hongling. The laughter grew more raucous, and someone shouted, 'Hongling, that's the second time you've been hit today by a mah-jong tile. The next time it'll kill you!' Hongling and Jade chased each other around the cellar knocking things over.

'Don't you worry, Hongling,' said Jade, 'tomorrow evening I'll get meat for you to eat. I promise I'll procure that nice Yangzhou Fabio for you and then your celibacy won't stop you from going to sleep!'

Hongling made a gesture that the watching girls did not understand, though its lewdness was obvious because the cellar erupted in laughter, and Jade's ample flesh shook all over.

Yumo, looking distracted, sat on an overturned barrel with a cigarette in one hand and a bowl of wine in the other.

After Shujuan and Xiaoyu had been watching for a while, they changed their minds about who was the prettiest. Yumo was becoming more attractive by the minute in their eyes. She was not instantly dazzling but she grew on them and was not easy to forget. Her hair was so thick and heavy that her face seemed to grow smaller when it was undone. As for the shape of her face, it was not square or round or long, it was simply diminutive and she had a pointed chin which gave her a slight air of arrogance. The sort of arrogance that said, 'If you look down on me, then I'll look down on you.' She had big, dark eyes and such a rapt gaze she always made you wonder if she had seen something you had not. Her mouth was her weak point: it was thin and wide, a garrulous, bitter sort of mouth. It was surprising that someone who measured her words so carefully had a mouth like that. It gave her a harsh, even ruthless look. Zhao Yumo's greatest asset was that she did not behave as if she were a shameless slut. In fact, you could imagine her as a concubine or a young wife in a rich man's household. Or as the actress in one of the advertisements they showed in movie houses. She looked different now from when she arrived: she had changed into a violet cheongsam of flowered cotton, on top of which she wore a thick white woollen wrap-around coat decorated with a couple of pompoms. She had correctly judged their new situation, and now that she was on the girls' territory, she made herself neat and tidy. Whether she had done this to save her skin or in an attempt to be treated as an equal, Shujuan had no way of knowing.

Four

The next morning, the women in the cellar did not stir. George took them some porridge but could not wake them up. Then, after lunch, they appeared outside the refectory complaining that no one had brought them anything to eat and they were weak with hunger.

Fabio could see that his strictures were having no effect on them. He called Yumo, as their ringleader, into the refectory.

'This is your last warning,' he said. 'If you all come out of the cellar again, you won't be welcome here any more.'

Yumo was apologetic. 'I understand that we're not welcome,' she said. 'But the women are really hungry.'

The prostitutes gathered around the refectory door to see whether their negotiator was doing a proper job or needed reinforcements.

'I'll come to food in a moment. First, I want to go over the rules once again,' Fabio said.

His efforts to turn his thick Yangzhou dialect into acceptable city speech caused some of the women a good deal of merriment.

'Talk about the toilet first, will you?' said Nani.

'We get nothing to eat and nowhere to crap!' complained Cardamom.

'There's a women's toilet in there,' said Hongling, pointing towards the workshop building. 'But the girls have locked it and they've got the key. We've only got the church to use –'

'You've been using the church toilets?' exclaimed Fabio. 'They're for the use of ladies and gentlemen of the congregation and their children during Mass! And the water's been cut off so they can't be flushed. They must smell terrible.'

Yumo fixed Fabio with enormous dark eyes. There was no avoiding her gaze and Fabio's heart skipped a beat.

When Fabio opened his mouth again, it was clear he had succumbed to the effects of Yumo's steady gaze. He pitched his voice lower and enumerated the arrangements: Ah Gu and George would dig a pit for them in the backyard and give them two tin buckets and two covers made from cardboard. When the buckets were full, they were to be emptied into the pit in the backyard. But that was to be done, he ordered them, before five o'clock in the morning so that they could avoid meeting the girls or Father Engelmann.

'Five o'clock in the morning?' exclaimed Hongling. 'But we don't usually get up until now.'

She raised a plump wrist and displayed a tiny watch on which the hour hand pointed to between one and two o'clock in the afternoon.

'From now on, you are to respect church hours, and get up and eat at church times. It's past breakfast time now, I'm sorry. The girls saved you a few scraps from their plates and you didn't eat them. They couldn't let noodles go to waste, could they?' As Fabio talked, he realised in surprise that he and Yumo were conducting a calm, polite conversation.

'Hah! Now we're really going to become nuns!' said Hongling with a laugh.

The allusion was obvious and the women chuckled. There was an edge in their laughter and even Fabio, who knew little of matters between men and women, was aware they were being lewd. 'Quiet! I haven't finished speaking,' he commanded harshly, although part of the harshness was directed at himself for no longer being sufficiently stern with them.

Yumo turned towards the women and quelled them with a glance.

'How many meals do we get a day?' asked Cardamom.

'How many would you like, Miss?' Fabio asked scornfully.

'Well, we usually get four meals, with an extra one at night-time,' Cardamom answered in all seriousness.

'Something simple at night would be fine,' Hongling hastily added, 'a few snack dishes, a soup, a nice glass of wine . . .' She knew Fabio was going to lose his temper. In fact, she thought he was very amusing when he was angry. In her experience, a fight between a man and a woman created instant intimacy and made everything more exciting.

'Can we join the congregation?' asked Nani.

Hongling clapped her hands in joy. 'So we've got someone here who wants to be baptised and made into a new person, have we? What she's actually asking is how many glasses of red wine can a person have when they go to Mass. Don't be taken in! She can drink a barrel of wine dry!'

'Bitch!' Nani swore at her but without any real anger.

Yumo hastily attempted to distract Fabio from their bad language. Fixing her gaze on him again, she said, 'Deacon Adornato, if it were not for your goodness in taking us in, we would all be facing calamity by now. We are deeply grateful that you are prepared to share a bowl of gruel with women like us in times of war. We would also like you to convey our thanks to the schoolgirls.'

Fabio felt drawn into the depths of those great eyes. Just for those few moments, he forgot that this woman was a whore, and imagined that she was someone he had come across in a park, or by the Xuanhu Lake, or in the shade of the French plane trees on Zhongshan Avenue; someone obviously from a good background. Perhaps she overdid the dignity a little, but her refinement and gentleness were genuine, and her words seemed honest, even if her accent was sometimes difficult to understand.

Fabio had planned to deal with the entire matter in a few brief sentences but he found himself leading Yumo round to the back of the church. Yumo was sharp-eyed and spotted the other women creeping after them. She stopped. 'Be good girls and go back to the cellar now. Fabio asked me to go with him, not all of you.'

Behind the church, there was a rectangular cistern built of carved white marble. A layer of hickory leaves, rotted to a rusty red, covered the bottom. Fabio pointed to the tea-coloured water which half filled the pond and said, 'I just wanted you to see this. Since you arrived, the water level has gone right down. Could I ask you to tell them not to pilfer the remaining water for washing clothes or faces?'

He felt ashamed of himself. Deep down he knew that he hadn't needed to bring her here alone to admonish her. He had just wanted to spend more time in her company, to drown himself in her black eyes. In fact, her eyes seemed to present a more terrible danger to him than the war outside the church walls.

'Of course, I'll pass on your message, Father,' Yumo said with a slight smile.

Her smile terrified him. She had divined thoughts in his head that he had scarcely divined himself. But it was also comforting. It said: It doesn't matter, you're a man, and you've shown you're made of flesh and blood.

'If the water supply stays cut off, within three days we'll die of thirst. We'll be as dry as this grass,' said Fabio, putting his foot on the lawn, which was withered and yellow from the winter drought. He sounded bitter, he thought, although he had not meant to.

'Was there ever a well here?' asked Yumo.

'Yes, but there was such heavy snowfall one year that Father Engelmann's pony missed its footing and slipped into the well. It broke its front leg. Father Engelmann made Ah Gu fill it in after that,' said Fabio.

'Can it be dug out again?'

'I don't know. It would be a lot of work. By the time we've used up the rest of the water in the cistern, maybe the water supply will be back on.' As he spoke, he told himself that once he had finished this sentence their conversation must end there.

Yumo seemed to have heard even that unspoken warning to himself. Smiling, she made a slight bow and said, 'I mustn't take up any more of your time.'

'If the situation gets any worse, and there's still no water, I really don't know what we'll do.' Somehow Fabio found himself leaving Yumo with another sentence. He hoped Yumo would take it as a muttered exclamation which had burst out despite himself, and would say goodbye. But she took it as the beginning of another exchange between them.

'It can't get worse. If it does, we'll go out and fetch

buckets of water. On our way here, we saw a pond,' she said.

'Strange that I don't remember a pond,' he said, telling himself this really was the very last thing he would say. Even if she said something more, he would not answer her.

'I remember it.' Another knowing smile. All men liked hanging around her, especially a lonely man like this one. The moment she set eyes on him, she had seen just how lonely Fabio was. No one accepted him as one of their own. He was alien both to the race into which he had been born and to the one in which he had grown up.

Fabio nodded, looking at her.

Yumo took a few steps, then stopped and turned round. 'Last night, we took a bet,' she said, 'about which side you'd be on if the Chinese and foreigners had a fight.'

'Which do you think?' asked Fabio.

She looked at him, smiling, then turned to go.

Sorceress! Fabio thought fiercely. As Yumo's elegant back receded into the distance, he vowed that he would never allow her to enthral him with those great dark eyes, even for a second.

* * *

That night, an icy sleet made the temperature plunge. Father Engelmann was reading in his study but felt chilled to the marrow in spite of the fire that burned in the fireplace in the library next door. The damage to the church tower meant that the first-floor rooms were extremely draughty. George made frequent trips to add wood to the fire but it seemed to make no difference. The next time George came up, Father Engelmann said, 'We'd better go easy on the wood. There isn't enough to go round, and many old people in the Safety Zone have frozen to death.'

Around midnight, unable to sleep, he returned to the library to find something else to read. When he got to the foot of the stairs, he heard women's voices. These women are like a virus, he thought. If you weren't careful, they spread everywhere. When he got to the door, he saw Yumo, Nani and Hongling huddled around the embers which glowed in the fireplace, holding out a garish assortment of underwear to dry in the warmth and giggling in low voices.

Here! In this place full of sacred books and holy pictures!

Father Engelmann's jaw muscles went into spasm. Convinced that these women would pay no attention when he rebuked them, he called Fabio from his bedroom.

'Fabio! What are these creatures doing here?'

Fabio, who had been drinking heavily, had just nodded off. The alcohol fuelled his fury. 'Blasphemers! How dare you come in here? Do you know what this place is?' he yelled.

'We're so cold down there, we've got chilblains. Look!' And Hongling pulled her bare feet with their painted toenails from her shoes and held them up before the two clergymen. Seeing Fabio jerk backwards as if she was contagious, Nani chortled in glee. Yumo elbowed her sharply; she knew they were in trouble now. This was the first time the distinguished old priest had really lost his composure.

'Let's go,' she said, hiding away the brassiere she was holding. Her face was burning hot, her back icy cold.

'I'm not going!' said Hongling. 'There's a fire in here. Why go back and freeze to death?'

She turned her back on the clergymen and stretched her bare feet towards the fireplace. She wriggled her toes as if her feet were talking in sign language.

'If you don't get out of here this instant, I'll make you all leave the church immediately!' said Fabio.

'And how will you make us do that?' asked Hongling, her big toe managing to be both mischievous and provocative.

Yumo grabbed her arm. 'Just stop that! Come on!'

'You want us to leave? It's easy! Give us a big brazier.'

'George!' Father Engelmann could see a shadow wavering at the bend of the staircase. George Chen had come over to see what was happening but, deciding it was best to stay out of trouble, was sneaking off down the stairs.

'I saw you! George, come here!'

George came in reluctantly and took in the scene at a glance. 'Father, have you not gone to bed yet?' he asked innocently.

'I asked you to put the fire out. Did you not understand?' Father Engelmann said, pointing at the fireplace.

'I was just about to,' said George.

'You've obviously added more wood!' said Father Engelmann.

'But George can't bear to see a nice woman like me freeze,' said Hongling with a twinkle in her eye.

Five

Outside, in the dark and the cold, a Chinese soldier pulled his greatcoat tightly around him and tried, in vain, to sleep. For the past two days he had been hiding in the church's graveyard, surviving on strips of dried yam that he had found hanging under the eaves of a bombed building, and on water from the cistern.

The soldier was twenty-nine-year-old Major Dai, of the Second Regiment of the 73rd Division of the Nationalist Army. On the night of December 12, while everyone in the compound slept, exhausted by their failed attempt to board the ferry, Dai had climbed over the wall into the church grounds in a desperate search for safety.

Major Dai's unit was part of a crack division which Chiang Kai-shek had used against the Japanese in Shanghai. Chiang Kai-shek had three regiments of the calibre of the Seventy-Third, and they were the jewels in his crown. The military instructor for all three divisions was General von Falkenhausen, a German aristocrat with a German temperament to match. The troops that had almost succeeded in driving the Japanese Army into the Huangpu River in the space of a week were Major Dai's.

On the evening of the twelfth, Major Dai was prepared to take half a battalion and defend Nanking's Central Road to the death. As it got dark, they came across large numbers of soldiers running in the direction of the river. The soldiers spoke an almost incomprehensible dialect but Dai gathered that, according to them, his commanding officer, General Tang, had called a meeting of senior officers that afternoon and decided on a general retreat to the river. They said the order to retreat had been given an hour ago.

This could not be true, Dai thought. There had been no order to retreat received from his runner. If Major Dai's crack troops had not received such orders, then what had made this rabble decide to throw away their weapons, bury their munitions and retreat?

Those in favour and those against retreat then got involved in discussions that became so acrimonious shots were fired. One of Dai's company captains was pushed to the ground by a retreating soldier and, when he got to his feet, he shot the man. At that, those under orders to defend the city split into two. Most were swept along by the retreating forces. Twenty or thirty soldiers were left and, taking advantage of the fact that they were still armed and the retreating forces had laid down their weapons, launched an attack on them. After about five minutes of being fired on, the retreating officers and men took refuge in tanks and lorries. Major Dai and his men blockaded the vehicles. In those few moments of pandemonium, it dawned upon Major Dai with terrible clarity what the word 'rout' meant. For a military man such as he was, doomsday could not have been more tragic than this. He gave the order to cease fire.

By the time he and his junior officers arrived at the river, it was a desperate scene: bloodied bodies crammed the banks, hands emerged from the water to cling to the gunwales of every boat. Dai's officers escorted him up and down, proclaiming his rank and number, but no one heeded them and they could not get near the few remaining boats which could take them to safety. By one o'clock in the morning, those wanting to board outnumbered those on the boats by a hundred to one. Innumerable hands still clung to the gunwales, and even the decks, with inhuman persistence, until the captain threatened to hack them off.

Dai decided this was futile. The river was now filled not just with motor boats and rowing boats, but wooden bathtubs, camphorwood chests and scrubbing boards. People, out of their minds with desperation, were prepared to risk the dangers of the river and try to paddle their tubs and boards to the opposite shore and safety. Dai reckoned that the first contingent must already have gone to a watery grave in the icy river. He and his officers turned and squeezed their way back through the crowds.

It was now four o'clock in the morning. The road was still jammed with fleeing soldiers and civilians. One soldier was trying to wrest a thin, patched and tattered cotton gown and trousers off one man, in exchange for his own army uniform, but the man would not give them up even though he was barefoot and unable to speak from the cold. Major Dai's shouted command went unheard and the soldier who desperately wanted to pass himself off as a Nanking shop-keeper would have ended up as another victim of 'friendly fire' had Dai not wanted to hang on to his remaining five bullets.

Dai groped his way through the unlit alleyways. Any buildings still standing were locked and barred. He came to an almost totally destroyed compound with a charred entrance door, walked in and found strings of yam strips hung from the eaves to dry. He cut them all down and filled his pockets with them.

He headed in what his memory of the layout of Nanking told him was an easterly direction. Most of the enemy troops had come from the east and if he could slip through to their rear and get into villages which had already surrendered, then he could hide away in these sparsely populated areas. From there he could plan the next step. It was not only knowledge and experience which made a soldier, it was natural aptitude, something Dai had in abundance and which was the reason why, at twenty-nine, he had been promoted over his peers so speedily at Baoding Military Academy.

Dai came across the first Japanese invaders at about five in the morning. This small group of soldiers appeared to have come in search of food, and were torching every house where they found none. When they arrived at the compound where Dai was hiding, he retreated to the innermost courtyard. Then he discovered that there were only half a dozen of them; he began to itch to have a go at them. A hand grenade was probably enough to deal with them. He would be a hopeless son of a bitch if he did not put his weapons to good use. Dai felt the grenade which hung from the rear of his waistband and pondered whether it was worthwhile. He did not hesitate long. A good soldier had not just knowledge, experience and ability, but also the kind of fervour which drove him into action. And Dai was seized now with the same burning hatred of the Japanese which had filled him when he fought them in Shanghai.

His heart pounding, he hid himself in the main hall of the innermost courtyard. There was a narrow alley outside the window, which he had opened and could get out of in a matter of seconds. Now he was really fired up, his frustration at the loss of Nanking completely forgotten.

The Japanese soldiers arrived in the inner courtyard and came into view. He held the pistol in one hand and, with his teeth, pulled the pin out of the grenade, silently counted to three, and then lobbed it out on the count of four. He was anxious not to waste any of the explosives he had, so the grenade had to land in the best possible position. As he threw it, he turned and hurled himself at the window. With the benefit of all his hard training, it took no more than a couple of seconds to scale the wall and land on the other side.

But the Japanese were also well trained. They had not been seriously wounded and were soon at the back windows themselves. Bullets hit the tree trunk to the left of him and the crumbling wall to the right. Then he realised one had hit him in his left side.

There was a high wall in front of him on the other side of the alley and the light from nearby fires lit up a cross atop a building inside. This must be an American church, he thought. The only way to get into the church grounds was by climbing the plane tree. He scaled its much-scarred trunk, and with each pull up, the wound in his left side oozed a spurt of blood.

When he got to the top of the wall, he saw seven or eight crosses. This was a graveyard, planted with poplars and holly, and Dai's eye fell on a building which looked like a small temple. He dived underneath the dome, sat down, undid his buttons and took out his first-aid kit. He probed his side but could not feel a bullet. This was much better than he had imagined. Now he just needed to staunch the wound. He was bleeding freely into his jacket and its sodden weight quickly turned icy cold.

He bound up the wound, his teeth chattering uncontrollably from the cold. This foreign 'temple' was a perfect, miniature mausoleum. If he died here, he would be dying among strangers, he thought.

When it got light, he discovered he had slept a little.

Then he heard female voices. What were women doing here?

Six

Shujuan looked into her bowl. Each day the soup seemed to get thinner. She was convinced it was because George was giving extra food to the Qin Huai women.

While the girls were eating their meal, the young prostitute Cardamom came into the refectory. She knew what they thought of her and made no attempt at good manners, shuffling across the old floorboards in her embroidered shoes.

'You've got soup!' she said.

The girls gave her a look designed to stop the most thick-skinned woman in her tracks. It didn't work on Cardamom.

'We only got given two loaves. They're really dry,' she complained.

No one paid any attention. George had made four loaves. The sixteen girls, the two clergymen, George and Ah Gu had made do with two of them so that the prostitutes could have the rest.

'She's got dry bread, and now she wants soup?' they thought. 'Does she think she's part of the family?'

'Do you really eat bread every day?' Cardamom asked. 'I'm just a country girl. Foreign bread disagrees with me.' She sidled over to the soup pot which sat on the table. There was only a little left in the bottom, a few overcooked strips of cabbage and scraps of noodle. Cardamom grew bolder and picked up the ladle. The handle was at right angles to the spoon, so you had to lift the handle straight up as if drawing water from a well. Cardamom couldn't manage it and the soup kept spilling out of the ladle and back into the pot. The girls carried on eating as if she was not there.

'Is anyone going to help me?' she asked with an impudent smile that made dimples in her cheeks.

'Someone should call Deacon Adornato,' one of the girls said.

'He's already been called,' said another.

Cardamom wasn't deterred. With her lips pursed and her eyes unblinking, she concentrated on learning how to get the soup from the pot into her bowl. 'Big deal,' she muttered. 'I'll learn the trick without your help.'

She was too short for the tall pot set on the tabletop, so she stood on her toes and drew the ladle up shakily. Even if she lifted the handle above her head, she still couldn't get the ladle out of the pot.

'The table's too tall,' she said.

'The dwarf complains about the table,' a schoolgirl quipped.

'I've seen taller winter melons,' said another.

'*You* are a winter melon!' Cardamom snapped back. She'd had enough. She dropped the ladle back into the pot with a hollow clatter.

'A rotten winter melon,' a third schoolgirl said.

'Step up and have a cursing match with me!' said Cardamom. '*If* you have the guts!'

No one wanted to pick a fight. That would be giving the slut more of their attention than she deserved. They carried on silently and soberly with their dinner. But when Cardamom turned to leave, someone piped up, 'More rotten than a winter melon in July. No one but the flies would want it!'

It was Xiaoyu.

'Stinks, doesn't she?' added Sophie.

Cardamom turned round. She walked over to where Sophie was sitting, picked up Sophie's bowl and flung the dregs of her soup in her face.

Sophie leapt out of her chair, dripping with cabbage leaves and bits of noodle. She hurled herself at Cardamom while Xiaoyu pulled Cardamom's foot. It took several of them to pin the young prostitute down. Shujuan went over to shut the door and wedged her back against it so that neither Fabio nor George could come in. Then all the girls crowded round the thrashing forms on the floor, aiding their friends by landing a kick or a pinch where they could. The Japanese were still abstract enemies, but this teenage prostitute was an enemy they could see.

*   *   *

Cardamom's shrill swearing percolated through the closed door and reached as far as Fabio's ears. He made his way to the refectory, too slowly for George's liking.

'They've been beating her up, Father. Something terrible's going to happen!' George exclaimed.

When they finally got the door open, they found Cardamom with her face covered in blood and a hank of her hair pulled out. She was rubbing a bald spot the size of a large coin on her head; it gleamed in the candlelight. George ran over to help her up, but she pushed him away and got to her feet unaided.

'I've had beatings since I was a kid,' she said to the girls through gritted teeth. 'I've had sticks broken over my backside. Your weak little fists are neither here nor there. What kind of people do you think you are anyway, all picking on me at once?'

The girls were paper-pale and tearful, as if they were the ones who had been injured. They all piped up at once: 'She started it! It was her fault!'

'Are any of you hurt?' Fabio asked, his eyes checking their faces.

They looked at him. Of course they were hurt. They were deeply wounded. All those filthy words the young whore had uttered had sullied innocent ears more used to Father Engelmann's resounding homilies, to music played on the church organ, to the classical poetry recited in their classes. The words forced an answer to their vague wonder about what happened between a man and a woman.

Fabio asked George to escort Cardamom back to the cellar. In a few minutes he was back, to say that Zhao Yumo was asking to speak to Deacon Adornato.

'No!' shouted Fabio, startling himself with the brusqueness of his response. As he saw George's surprised expression he realised how abrupt he must have sounded. He turned and headed in haste towards the rectory. *You think you can seduce me with a pair of pretty eyes, do you, Yumo?* he thought to himself. *You think I'll come running when you call? We've got to get rid of those women. I'll petition Father Engelmann to get them into the Safety Zone one way or another.*

Fabio's footsteps suddenly slowed, as he came to the anguished realisation that he could not steel himself to do it.

When Fabio Adornato was a boy of six, his missionary parents had died of plague while away on a trip. But the woman who had been a true mother to him was his Chinese 'granny'. (Though 'granny' was only a manner of speaking, as actually she was only a few years older than his parents.) It was she who had looked after him since birth, and carried him around all day on her back. It was her soft, flaccid breasts which had been his haven when he was a little boy, which would send him to sleep as soon as he nestled into them. After his parents died, his real, American granny came to China to reclaim him. She was a tall woman with a mass of curly hair, dressed from head to toe in black. He hid behind his Chinese granny and refused to come out to be introduced to her. She had come to take him back to America, she said, via the painful interpreting of a Chinese teacher in the local town. As soon as Fabio heard this awful news, he made his escape.

The rice had just been harvested and there were plenty of straw stacks to hide in. At nightfall he sneaked back to his Chinese granny's thatched hut and pulled down some dried water chestnuts and rice cakes which she stored by hanging them under the eaves. These he took back to the straw stack to eat. The old woman had a dozen or so speckled ducks and Fabio knew exactly where they laid their eggs. He supplemented the chestnuts and rice cakes by going to the place before she went to the river to collect the eggs, stealing a couple, cracking them open and eating them raw. She complained that her things went missing and that someone was stealing them, but she knew perfectly well who it was. Why should an old widow like her not be a bit selfish? She wanted to hang on to Fabio.

His grandmother sorted out her daughter and son-in-law's

possessions, and sold off their furniture and clothing. Then she waited in vain for Fabio to come back. Finally, she could not bear village food, houses, toilets and mosquitoes any more and gave up the idea of taking her grandson home with her. She asked the clan head in the village to tell the Chinese teacher in the local town that as soon as Fabio was found he should write to her in English and she would come back and collect him. But Fabio's grandmother never received any further news of her grandson from the village.

When Fabio grew up, he came secretly to regret his youthful intransigence but that was after he had been taken in as a seminarist by Father Engelmann. When his American grandmother left, his Chinese granny had thrown herself and Fabio on the mercy of one of her distant relatives. The man was a friend of Fabio's parents and had introduced his granny to them so she could help around the house and with the boy. Now he took in Fabio's granny to do the laundry and cleaning and brought the boy up with his own children. When Fabio, at seventeen, graduated from the missionary middle school, Father Engelmann happened to be there lecturing. The priest was intrigued by this young man, who talked and behaved like a Chinese but had the body of a Westerner, and made a point of talking to him. When he left Yangzhou to return to Nanking, it was Fabio Adornato who carried his baggage for him because, from the moment Father Engelmann had stepped down from the pulpit and come towards him with a smile on his face, Fabio knew that the reason why he had been so lonely all his young life was that he would never be Chinese. It was as much Father Engelmann's air of refinement and calm as his eloquence and the depth of his knowledge which, within a very short time, tamed Fabio and brought him to the realisation that he did not even want to be Chinese. He also understood that Father Engelmann was drawn to him because he was a Westerner. His new mentor hinted to him that it was beneath Fabio's dignity to continue to mix with Chinese people as a Chinese man. Father Engelmann and Fabio stood out from the crowd like a pair of camels who had met by chance in a herd of horses. It was if they had known each other for years.

When Fabio graduated from the Nanking Seminary, Father Engelmann, who did some teaching there, applied for a scholarship for his protégé so that he could continue his studies in America for a further three years. In America Fabio managed to trace his entire American family, young and old. But being with them made him so anxious, he began to itch and scratch his head frantically. He realised that he could not be an American either. The friendly chit-chat with his American relatives was just a front. The real Fabio retreated into the recesses of his heart and counted the seconds until this momentous reunion with his blood relatives could come to an end.

Fabio walked across the lawn to the rectory. When he reached Father Engelmann's door, he knocked lightly.

'Come in.'

Father Engelmann and Fabio were on good terms, the same good terms that they had been on since they first met, neither more intimate nor more distant. That was the kind of person Father Engelmann was. If he was your neighbour, he would greet you genially the first time with a 'How good to meet you!' And when you had been neighbours for decades, he would still greet you with the same 'How good to meet you!' He was able to freeze-frame familiarity so that it neither matured nor died.

'Is something the matter, Fabio?' he said now. He did not ask Fabio to sit down with his usual civility.

The priest was hunched over his short-wave radio listening to overseas broadcasts on the situation in Nanking. He glanced round at Fabio, then turned back to his radio.

Fabio was silent and listened with him to the crackly broadcast. He realised it was not the moment to talk to the priest about something as trivial as women fighting over food.

He glanced at the pale rectangular and oval marks of varying sizes on the faded walls where framed pictures had once hung. When the air raids first started, Father Engelmann had made Ah Gu take the pictures down and store them in the cellar, in case the glass shattered during a raid. Fabio remembered each of the pictures even in their absence, because Father Engelmann had not changed or moved them around in decades. The vertical oval outline, the largest, was a portrait photo of his mother, taken from a tiny photo on the back of a pocket watch his father had left him, and enlarged and touched up to such an extent that it was as much a product of science as of art. Below it on the left, the rectangular shape marked where a full-length graduation photo had hung, the only evidence of Father Engelmann ever having been young. On the bottom right, the horizontal oval was where the picture of Father Engelmann with His Holiness Pope Pius XI used to hang.

'It seems it's true,' Father Engelmann muttered. 'They've secretly executed Chinese soldiers. The shots I heard came from the execution ground by the river. Even the Japanese reporters and the Germans were shocked.'

The gunfire had made Father Engelmann wonder whether Chinese troops were still resisting. He had been told by officials in the Safety Zone that any troops who had not had time to retreat had been taken prisoner. But the gunfire he had heard and the news from the wireless seemed to contradict this.

'Are the Japanese really flouting international rules on the treatment of prisoners of war?' he said to Fabio. 'That's an affront to all civilised, humane values. Can you believe it? Are these really the same Japanese people I know?'

'We need to find a way to get food and water. Otherwise, by tomorrow there won't be any drinking water,' said Fabio.

Father Engelmann understood what Fabio was getting at: there was absolutely no sign that, within the hoped-for few days, the invading forces would stop the butchery, take control of the vanquished city and impose law and order. Moreover, the killing had become a habit, and the prospect of it stopping seemed remote. There was something else Fabio was getting at: very soon, they would all suffer the consequences of Father Engelmann's generosity in taking in the prostitutes and allowing them to deprive the school-girls of their food.

'I'll go to the Safety Zone tomorrow and get hold of some food – potatoes, yams or whatever. If that can keep us going for another two days, at least the children won't starve,' Engelmann said.

'And what about after that?' asked Fabio. 'And what about water?'

'We have to take it hour by hour now! Getting through another hour is another hour of life!'

Fabio felt furious. Father Engelmann repeatedly criticised him for passive aggression, telling him that disagreements should be thrashed out openly and confrontation should be direct. That was the way almost all Americans behaved. Fabio's passive aggression was a Chinese trait, one which he, Father Engelmann, deplored.

Now he looked at Fabio and asked, 'With regard to water, have you any constructive suggestions to make?'

'Zhao Yumo said that when they came here, they passed a pond on the way. I know Nanking pretty well, and I don't remember one nearby, but she said she saw it. I thought I'd ask Ah Gu to go and look for it before it gets light.'

'That's a very good idea of yours. You see, we've already

found a way around the problem.' And Father Engelmann rewarded Fabio with a warm smile, very different from his usual polite, cold smiles.

Fabio felt a rush of emotion. After all these years with Father Engelmann, he had now, in the space of ten minutes, been on the receiving end of real anger and a genuine smile from him. Perhaps it signalled that the distance Father Engelmann had been so careful to maintain over all this time just might be breaking down.

'Tell the children to go to the church,' said Father Engelmann.

'But they'll surely be asleep,' said Fabio.

'Go and tell them, please.'

Seven

The girls had gone to bed but fumbled for their clothes when they heard Fabio's shout and came down from the attic. They entered the church to see Fabio seated at the organ and Father Engelmann standing dressed in his funeral cassock. They felt something must be badly amiss and clutched each other's ice-cold hands for comfort. In an instant all the petty animosities and daily rivalries between them dissolved and they became a collective, a family.

The organist had gone, having left Nanking along with the other teachers, which was why Fabio was now playing. He had studied music for a year in the seminary and so knew the rudiments. It was an upright organ, normally used for teaching the girls to sing, and was now muffled in an old carpet which made the music sound nasal as if it had caught cold.

Someone must have died, thought Shujuan, and the organ had been wrapped up to keep the funeral hymns as quiet as possible. Or perhaps Father Engelmann knew what they had done to Cardamon and was about to make them repent. But Cardamom had deserved it. Surely he would understand that, and take their side.

The entire nave was lit with only three candles and all the windows were covered in blackout curtains, of the kind which covered all the windows of every building in Nanking now that there were air raids.

The organ growled and the girls sang the requiem in whispers. They did not know who the requiem was for, or who they had lost, but perhaps for that very reason they had the confused feeling that they were facing a vast infinity of loss: Nanking and south China; the right to be a free people; and something else besides.

Father Engelmann led them in prayer.

Shujuan looked at Father Engelmann standing in front of the figure of Christ. His shadow fell on the painted statue hanging from its cross, and his living face took on some of its ecstasy.

'Children, I did not want to alarm you but now I must prepare you for a greatly worsened situation,' the priest began. Then he quietly outlined for them in simple terms what the wireless broadcasts had said. 'If these reports, that hundreds and thousands of prisoners of war have been executed, are true then I believe that we must have returned to the Middle Ages. As Chinese, you will know that the Qin dynasty buried four hundred thousand Zhao kingdom prisoners of war alive. We do not seem to have advanced much since then.' Father Engelmann stopped speaking. His Chinese had become increasingly awkward and his words harder to understand.

* * *

That night, Shujuan and Xiaoyu lay side by side. Xiaoyu sobbed and sobbed and, when Shujuan asked her what the matter was, said that her father was a powerful man who could fix anything, yet he had left her to starve in this freezing hellhole.

'Well, my parents are in America, tucking into bacon and eggs and coffee,' said Shujuan.

Suddenly Xiaoyu shook her friend's arm hard and said, 'When my father comes to get me, I'll take you with me.'

'Do you think he'll come and get you?'

'Of course he will!' Xiaoyu seemed offended that Shujuan should be doubting her wealthy, all-powerful father.

'I hope he comes tomorrow,' said Shujuan, her eager anticipation of Xiaoyu's father as great as her friend's. What a wonderful thing to be Xiaoyu's best friend now, to bathe in the light which shone from her, to flee blockaded Nanking.

'Where do you want to go?' asked Xiaoyu.

'Wherever you're going.'

'Let's go to Shanghai. They won't attack the British, French and American concessions. Shanghai would be good, better than Hankou. Hankou would be death. It's all Chinese there.'

'Good. Shanghai it is then.' Shujuan did not dare contradict Xiaoyu. It was slightly degrading to have to depend on Xiaoyu in this way; still, it was only for now. She had all her life ahead of her in which to rebuild her self-esteem.

There was a faint ring of the doorbell. In seconds, all the girls were sitting upright and then clustered around the windows. They saw Ah Gu and Fabio race out of the door beneath their windows. Ah Gu, a lantern in his hand, was there first. Fabio caught up and gestured fiercely at Ah Gu that he should extinguish the light. But it was too late. The light had already filtered through the crack in the door to the outside.

'Please, sirs, open the door, I'm a gravedigger . . . This soldier is still alive . . .'

'Please go away,' Fabio said laboriously in awkward Chinese. 'This is an American church. We don't get involved in fighting between Chinese and Japanese soldiers.'

'Please, sir, save me!' came another voice. It sounded very weak, as if the man was seriously wounded.

'Please go away. I'm very sorry.'

The gravedigger raised his voice. 'The Japanese will be back any moment now! Then he'll be dead and so will I! Please show mercy to us. I'm a Christian too!'

'Please take him to the Safety Zone,' said Fabio.

'The Japs go to the Safety Zone dozens of times every day to pick up Chinese soldiers and the wounded! Please, I beg you!'

'I'm very sorry. It's quite impossible. Please don't force me to compromise the neutrality of this church.'

Gunshots were heard from somewhere nearby.

The gravedigger refused to give up. 'Merciful priests,

I beg you!' Then his footsteps were heard receding into the distance. He had clearly left the wounded soldier behind.

Fabio did not know what to do. He could not let the Chinese soldier outside bleed to death, but neither could he put the nearly forty souls inside at risk.

At that moment, Father Engelmann suddenly emerged out of the darkness, still wearing his funeral cassock.

'What's happening?' he asked Fabio and Ah Gu.

'There's a seriously wounded soldier outside,' said Fabio. 'Should we bring him in?'

For the first time since he had met Father Engelmann, Fabio sensed that the priest had no idea what to do.

'Please, I beg you!' The wounded man outside spoke through clenched teeth.

'We have to open up,' said Fabio in English. 'If he dies outside our door, we'll be compromised.'

Engelmann looked at his junior. He knew Fabio was right, but he dared not contemplate the prospect of losing the church's neutrality, and thus losing their ability to protect the schoolgirls. 'We can't,' he said. 'But we could get Ah Gu to take him away and leave him in some other place.'

'That would be sending him to his death!' exclaimed Ah Gu.

Outside the door, the wounded man gave a groan which sounded scarcely human.

From where Shujuan stood at the window the two clergymen in their black robes and Ah Gu looked like three figures on a chessboard. She watched Father Engelmann take the key from Ah Gu and undo the sturdy German-made lock. He pushed the bolts to one side and pulled the chain free. The door opened heavily and the girls gave a sigh of relief.

But then, even faster and more firmly than he had opened it, Father Engelmann shut the door again before anyone outside could get in. He attempted to lock up again, but his movements were clumsy. Fabio asked him what was going on. Engelmann said nothing and concentrated instead on locking and bolting the door.

'There's not one but two outside. Two wounded Chinese soldiers!' he said in aggrieved tones.

There was another shout from the gravedigger. 'The Japs are coming! On horses!'

It was clear that he had only pretended to go away. He had correctly gambled on the assumption that the foreign monks would not leave a lone wounded man to bleed to death. Father Engelmann had fallen into the trap, and opened the door. The gravedigger had said there was only one casualty because he feared that the church would not take in more than one.

'I really can hear horses!' said Ah Gu.

Even Shujuan knew that if a Japanese soldier on horseback were to turn into the alleyway outside the church, then that would be the end of them all, both inside and outside.

'Why did you lie to me? There's clearly more than one casualty!' shouted Father Engelmann. 'You Chinese do nothing but tell lies, even at a time like this!'

'Father, we're saving lives. What does it matter if it's one or one hundred?' said Fabio. This was the first time he had directly confronted his mentor.

'You shut up,' said Father Engelmann.

The men outside did not understand the foreigners' conversation but they knew it had to do with whether they lived or died. The gravedigger became frantic and shouted, 'The horses are coming this way!'

Father Engelmann walked back the way he had come, the key in his hand. He had only gone half a dozen paces when a dark figure swiftly blocked his way. It appeared to be that of a soldier.

Sophie, who was standing next to Shujuan, gave a yelp

like a puppy. The war had arrived here and their compound was going to be a battlefield.

The intruder closed in on Father Engelmann. 'Open up!' he ordered. The conflagration from a distant building seemed to have set the sky on fire, and the light from it flickered across the courtyard. The girls could see that the soldier was holding a pistol to Father Engelmann's chest, no doubt making the priest's heart thump under his black cassock. If the soldier were even a little sensitive, Shujuan thought, he must surely be aware of that thudding heart.

Fabio took the key from Father Engelmann's hand and opened the door. In came a little group of people, one of whom lay covered in blood in a wheelbarrow. The one who had been talking through the door was using a roughly cut tree branch as a crutch. The wheelbarrow was being pushed by a middle-aged man wearing a black waistcoat.

Not long after the door was shut again, some Japanese cavalry rode down the street, laughing and singing cheerfully.

Everyone inside stood motionless as statues until the Japanese had passed. The soldier in uniform still held the pistol in both hands, the bullets ready to fly if the door should be opened again. Not until the echoes of the horses' hooves had faded into the distance did they relax.

'Let's go down and have a look,' Shujuan whispered to Xiaoyu.

'You can't!' exclaimed Xiaoyu.

'Come on, it's easy.'

Xiaoyu's face suddenly became hard. 'You go alone, Shujuan. And don't count on me to save your skin.'

Shujuan opened the trapdoor, the ladder extended beneath her and she set off on her own.

'Look at Shujuan!' she heard Xiaoyu say to the other girls. 'She's always looking for trouble!'

Shujuan was furious with Xiaoyu. She had intended to sneak away with her friend behind the backs of the others, and now Xiaoyu had betrayed her to them.

She crept down to the entrance to the workshop building and pushed open the door a crack so that she could see what was happening outside. She was not a girl who liked the wool pulled over her eyes. She knew it was just a way of protecting her but she did not appreciate it at all.

Through the crack in the door, she could see that the struggle in the courtyard was still unresolved. The wheelbarrow had taken on the role of the tank, creaking over the ground as the soldier wielding the pistol led their advance. Shujuan could see that the man wearing the strange black waistcoat had white cloth circles stuck to the front and back; she supposed this was the normal garb for gravediggers.

'Ah Gu, go and get the first-aid box,' ordered Father Engelmann. 'Give them a supply of swabs and dressings and get rid of them.' He was making it very clear he would not receive guests like this at the church.

The pistol-wielding soldier did not strike an aggressive posture but he still pointed the pistol at the priest as he said: 'Where do you want them to go to?'

'Please put your weapon down when you talk to me, Major,' Father Engelmann responded with dignity.

He had seen the man's rank. He had also seen that his jacket had a dark patch at the hem on the left-hand side where the blood had soaked through.

'Pardon me, Father,' said the soldier still pointing his gun.

'Are you trying to force me at gunpoint to take you all in?'

'People only listen when you've got a gun in your hand.'

'Why didn't you use your gun to make the Japanese listen to you?'

The soldier was silent.

'You see, Officer, I don't talk to people who are armed. Please put your gun down.'

The officer lowered his gun.

'Would you mind telling me who you are and how you got in?' Fabio asked him.

'It was easy. I've been here for days,' answered the soldier. 'I'm Major Dai Tao, second in command, Second Regiment, 73rd Division.'

At that point, a slight sound reached their ears.

Shujuan peered out and saw half a dozen women emerging from the kitchen with Hongling at their head. They certainly could not complain that they were 'bored to death' any more: before their eyes a blood-soaked bundle lay in a wheelbarrow. They stopped and began to whisper among themselves. They appeared to realise for the first time that the peace of this compound was a mirage, as false as their constant chatter and laughter. The reality was that the rivers of blood in the city outside had finally reached the church walls.

'How many did the Japanese kill?' asked Major Dai, looking at the soldier lying wounded in the wheelbarrow and then over to the sergeant major supporting himself on a makeshift crutch

'Five or six thousand,' said the sergeant major with the crutch in tones of angry humiliation. 'They hoodwinked us! Those fucking Japs said they were taking us to clear land for crops on an island in the river, but when we got to the riverbank, we couldn't see a single boat –'

'Are you from the 154th Division?' Dai interrupted sharply.

'Yes. How did you know?' asked the sergeant major.

Major Dai did not answer. The dialect the sergeant major spoke had told him all he needed to know. 'Find a warm place, and dress his wounds,' he said, in tones that indicated he had taken over the compound and was now in charge.

The sergeant major was about to obey when Father Engelmann said, 'Wait a moment. Major, I saved you all just now, but I can't do it again. There are sixteen teenage girls taking refuge here, and if I let soldiers stay, that'll be an excuse for the Japanese to break in too.' His laboured pronunciation in Chinese was certainly hard to understand.

'If they leave here, then they'll be shot again,' said the major.

Suddenly Hongling chipped in. 'Those murderous Japanese! . . . Officer, let them squeeze into our cellar!'

'No!' Father Engelmann roared.

'Father, can we dress their wounds first and then assess the situation?' Fabio said.

'No,' said Father Engelmann again. 'This is getting out of hand. We've run out of water and food, and now three extra people . . . please consider our schoolgirls, the oldest only fourteen. What would you do in my position? I think you'd do what I'm doing and refuse to let soldiers in here. Soldiers will encourage the Japanese to come here. Is that fair to the girls?' He enunciated the words with almost painful precision in an effort to make himself understood.

'But won't the Japanese come even if we're not here?' objected the sergeant major. 'There's nowhere they won't go!'

Father Engelmann hesitated. The sergeant major had a point. From what he had seen it was clear that, to these crazed invaders, nowhere was taboo, nothing was sacred.

He turned to Dai. 'Please understand my situation, Major, and take them away. May God protect you until you get to the Safety Zone, and God speed.'

'Push the wheelbarrow over there,' Dai said, pointing the gravedigger in the direction of the kitchen, as if he had not taken in a word of Father Engelmann's Chinese. 'Give them a little water and then let me take a look at their wounds.'

'Stay right where you are,' said Father Engelmann, blocking the way, his outstretched arms in the black cassock looking like two black wings.

Dai raised his gun again.

'Are you going to shoot? If so, the church will be yours and you can put the wounded wherever you want. Go on, shoot,' said the priest.

Dai pulled back the safety catch on the pistol.

Fabio's jaw dropped open but he stood stock-still. He was afraid that any movement might set the bullets flying.

The wounded man in the wheelbarrow moaned in agony. It was the high-pitched moan of a boy of fourteen or fifteen with a just-broken voice, one who sounded close to death. None of this wrangling about neutrality seemed to matter, even life and death itself seemed trivial, when right there in front of them there was a boy soldier suffering such pain.

'All right. Deal with the wounds and then we'll see,' Father Engelmann finally said.

'The hot water's ready!' said George, who had been waiting quietly while the arguments went on around him. He had said nothing but he had taken sides, and had begun preparing to help the wounded. Now the very last of the remaining water from the cistern was heating on the stove.

The women had all emerged from the cellar by this time. They stood staring mutely at the dying boy soldier and the wounded sergeant in either distaste or fear, it was hard to tell. They could have been a phalanx of funeral mourners, or greeters at a party.

Major Dai was about to follow them when Father Engelmann stopped him.

'Give me your gun, Major.'

The officer frowned. His expression said: *What does this foreigner think he's doing? The Japanese haven't managed to disarm me yet!*

'If you want the church's protection, then you must give up your weapon. The strength of this church lies in its neutrality, and we'll lose that the minute we take in people who are armed. So give me your gun.'

Major Dai looked into the priest's pale, foreigner's eyes and said, 'No.'

'Then I'm not letting you stay.'

'I won't be staying, at least no more than a day or two.'

'If you want to stay here for another minute, then it has to be as an ordinary citizen. If the Japanese discover you here with a weapon, I can't defend you and I can't defend the neutrality of the church either.'

'If the Japanese really get in, and I haven't got a weapon, then we'll be like lambs to the slaughter.'

'I can only give you refuge here as an ordinary citizen if you give up your weapon. Otherwise you must leave now.'

Major Dai hesitated, then he said: 'I'll just stay one night, long enough to debrief these two about the massacre of the prisoners of war. Then I'll go.'

'I told you. Not another minute.'

'Do as the Father says, Major,' put in Fabio. 'You're seriously wounded yourself. If you leave here, you'll be without food and water, and the Japanese are everywhere. How far will you get? At least get your wound treated and give yourself a bit of a rest and then go.' His Yangzhou accent had a persuasive force to it. He sounded as if he was trying to make two squabbling village boys see the error of their ways.

Slowly, Major Dai clicked on the pistol's safety catch. Then he turned the muzzle towards himself and gave the pistol, butt-end first, to Father Engelmann.

Eight

To maintain propriety, the cellar was divided in two with the aid of an old curtain from the library. The three men had one side, the women the other. As Fabio came down the ladder to inspect the arrangements, his nostrils were assaulted by an extraordinary medley of smells: foodstuffs stored for long years, pickles, cheese, wine ... their substance may have disappeared but their essence remained. It was as if the smells had continued to ripen until they filled the air with a pungent, almost tangible odour. Fabio felt faint as he got to the bottom of the ladder. New smells had been added to the mixture since this had become a makeshift living space: the body odour of fourteen women and three men, the contents of two toilet buckets, as well as perfume, face cream, hair oil, talcum powder and tobacco . . .

The sergeant major's name was Li Quanyou and the boy soldier was Wang Pusheng. Fabio learned that the boy had only been conscripted a month before, having been dragged from the sweet-potato patch in front of his house and handed a uniform. The day he put it on, he was given a rifle and a munitions belt and taken off to the village threshing circle to learn how to use his bayonet and take aim, before being sent to Nanking. He had not even had one chance to shoot his gun because his superior said bullets were worth their weight in gold and had to be kept until they got to the battlefield. Once there, he had fired only a few shots when he was wounded.

Sergeant Major Li's left leg was badly injured. He had been stabbed four times and the tendons behind the knee had been severed so that the limb looked dead as he dragged it uselessly behind him.

It took some probing for Major Dai to extract the story of what had happened to them. At first when he asked, Li just said: 'Don't want to talk about it. They're motherfuckers, I've never been in such a hellish situation!' Or: 'I just don't remember!' It was only after he'd had some wine that he started to tell the story. The wine, of course, belonged to the church and had been smuggled to the soldiers by the women. By that time, adversity had drawn the soldiers and the prostitutes into a close alliance.

Major Dai told the story to Fabio, who relayed it to Father Engelmann.

The day after Li Quanyou and Wang Pusheng's unit had sworn that they would defend the city to the last man, they had lost contact with their GHQ. As a result, their officers had no idea where to go or how to fight. They also did not know which direction the enemy was attacking from. It was only when the Japanese breached their lines and marched into Nanking that Li and his men realised they were defeated pawns in a chess game.

It was getting dark and Chinese and enemy troops became hopelessly mixed up. During the night, they were sold out by their own senior officers who, from the rank of captain upwards, simply ran away under cover of darkness. At dawn, a Chinese collaborator armed with a loud-hailer, speaking from a Japanese helicopter, announced: 'Chinese soldiers! The great Japanese Imperial Army treats its prisoners of war well! You only have to put down your arms, and rice, hot tea and Japanese Army tinned rations await you!' None of the Chinese soldiers had had so much as a sniff of rice for a very long time. As the Japanese helicopter circled around the mountains, the soldiers sheltering on its wooded slopes craned their necks to watch. When the helicopter returned, the collaborator had turned into a Japanese girl, singing a Chinese song in a Japanese accent. The helicopter circled again and the sky filled with white, yellow and pink leaflets fluttering to the ground. A soldier who could read a bit said: 'These are from the Japanese! They want us to surrender.' Others who were more literate read the rest of the text: 'It says there'll be no violence, and it guarantees us food and shelter. And it says any resistance will meet with total annihilation. All the Chinese troops inside Nanking have surrendered and are being treated well!' There was another leaflet whose wording was less polite: 'The patience of the Imperial Army is not inexhaustible. If you have not surrendered by dawn tomorrow, it will be too late.'

During the night the soldiers discussed their options. Sergeant Major Li suggested to one of his platoon commanders that they break ranks and escape under cover of darkness. They might be lucky and get away. But the platoon commander said: 'If you've thought of that idea, then the Japanese will have too.' Another sergeant said: 'If we take these leaflets with us, then if the Japanese don't keep their word, we can argue with them, because it's all down here in black and white! It's even got their senior officer's name written here. Would he dare go back on his word?'

The terms of surrender were printed on other leaflets: 1) they were to collect all their weapons into a pile; 2) they were to form up in their squads, platoons and companies and the head of each was to raise a white flag – a white sheet or a white shirt would do; 3) every officer and every man was to raise their hands above their heads and come out into the open. The Japanese Army wanted orderly behaviour. Any disorderly behaviour would be severely punished.

Li had no food on him at all but he did have tobacco. He filled pipe after pipe, trying to weigh up the odds and make up his mind: to surrender with the rest of the troops or attempt to sneak quietly away on his own. If he had a mouthful of food there was no way he would surrender. His comrades all got out their remaining tobacco and pooled it. The damp, cold night air seeped from the dense stands of pine and oak and chilled the many thousands of hungry Chinese soldiers to the bone. Only their tobacco brought them a little comfort.

At this very moment, although they did not know it, Japanese troops were watching the mass of dots of light from countless pipes in some trepidation. The Chinese looked like a mighty force and the Japanese were only a fraction of their number. If the leaflets ploy should fail, it would be hard for the Japanese to do battle with the Chinese.

Li finally abandoned the idea of fleeing and going into hiding. If he surrendered, at least he had a vague idea what would happen from the Japanese leaflets. If he made a run for it, he had no way of knowing what awaited him. Besides, when it came to trusting to fate, Li like most of his comrades preferred to stick with the others. Their courage was multiplied when they were together and a deadly threat was much easier to face together than alone.

At five o'clock in the morning, the first white flag – a bed sheet held aloft by a bugler – was raised on the Chinese side. The sheet had been left behind by a regimental commander. They tore it into four and shared it between four regiments. It was only when the mist lifted and the surrendering troops got to the Japanese lines that they realised just how heavily they outnumbered the enemy. If only they had known, they could have broken through and got away the night before, but the lack of any wireless equipment left them in complete ignorance, a situation which the Japanese were quick to take advantage of.

A group of walking wounded was approaching along another track. One of them was a youth with his head wrapped in a bandage. Li's company was ordered to halt at the fork in the track. The Japanese seemed to be very considerate of their prisoners of war, allowing the wounded to get to food and shelter first. Sergeant Major Li and Wang Pusheng had not met at that stage.

Led by a forest of white flags, the Chinese troops silently walked along the road. They were escorted at ten-metre intervals by a Japanese soldier toting a rifle. Occasionally Chinese interpreters would appear, to shout: 'Hurry up! Quick as you can!' Every now and then they would be asked by the surrendering soldiers: 'Where are the Japanese taking us?'

The answer was always 'Don't know'. The expressions of the collaborators were as bland as those of the Japanese soldiers escorting them.

'Will there be food and water?' came another question.

'Of course!'

'They won't kill us or beat us?'

'No! Get a move on now!'

There really were some soldiers who had carefully kept a leaflet on them. Every time they saw a collaborator, they would take it out and show it to him. These words were the evidence. Now they wanted these Japanese to honour their promises.

When one of the soldiers exchanged a few words with a collaborator, he was quickly surrounded by his comrades. 'They're really not going to kill us?' 'That's what he said . . .' 'They're going to feed us?' 'That's what he said . . .'

The rumours were embellished with much repeating. 'Down the road there's food! We're nearly there! The Japanese never kill their prisoners!'

They walked on and on but food and shelter still did not materialise. The prisoners' firmness of spirit began to waver. 'Who did you hear say there was food?' 'It was you!' 'Did I? I said probably there was . . .' 'Then let's find another interpreter to ask!'

It was after ten in the morning and the mist was dispersing when they came to a burned-out factory. A Japanese officer exchanged a few words with the interpreter who took a loud-hailer and bellowed at the prisoners: 'Officers and men! Take a rest here for a bit while we wait for our orders.'

One of the Chinese, bolder than the rest, shouted back: 'Is this where we're going to eat?'

The Japanese officer bent his steely gaze on him and the Chinese soldiers felt a chill of fear. There was obviously no food and shelter to be had here.

The place was completely uninhabited. It was a ghost town.

Under instruction from the Japanese officer, the interpreter addressed the prisoners again. 'There'll be food when you get to the river. Then you'll be put in boats and taken to an island in midstream to clear the land for planting. The Japanese Army needs food and you're going to supply it . . .'

The men were reassured when this message was relayed to them. It sounded believable. They could see the prospects in front of them. They might have been starving but they cheered up. The interpreter went on. 'During this rest period, we're asking everyone to show restraint and cooperate with the Japanese. Allow them to tie your hands –'

The loud-hailer was still rapping out its message when there were confused shouts of: 'Why? What do they want to tie our hands for?'

'They've got guns and we're weaponless. What's the point in tying us up?'

'I won't let them!'

The officer shouted an order and all the Japanese soldiers stood with bayonets at the ready.

The Chinese quieted down and huddled closer together.

The loud-hailer transmitted the Japanese officer's explanation. 'Tying your hands is to keep you in order. If we lose control and disorder breaks out when you're crossing the river, then it could be very dangerous. The Imperial Army is only concerned with your safety.'

The collaborator shouted himself hoarse through the loud-hailer but the soldiers were sceptical.

One shouted back: 'If they tie our hands, then how will we eat when we get to the river?'

The collaborator had no answer to that. But the question alerted the other soldiers: Hadn't the Japanese said they would be fed when they got to the river? So why were they saying now that tying their hands was to maintain order on the boats? How could they hold a bowl and pick up a steamed bun with their hands tied? And there were only a few Japanese – were there enough to get food to all the Chinese? Which bit were they to believe?

The Japanese officer moved over to the interpreter. 'What's all the noise about?' he asked. The interpreter smiled and explained to him that the things he had said contradicted each other.

The officer thought for a moment and had a muttered exchange with the interpreter. The latter turned back to the prisoners and raised his loud-hailer again. 'Chinese soldiers, the commanding officer acknowledges that you are right and his plan was ill-considered. So this is what we'll do: all of you will make camp here and when the food supplies department tells us they are ready, then you will be informed.'

Sergeant Major Li and his comrades were escorted into the empty factory. It was a tight squeeze for five thousand soldiers, and there was not an inch of extra space for anyone to stretch out and take a nap. But the prisoners were so exhausted and hungry that they simply fell asleep sitting bolt upright. As it got dark, they began to wake up but not a single man had the strength to stand.

Li was on the outside edge of the group. Just a couple of feet away, he saw a long bayonet. He followed the bayonet upwards until he got to a blank, expressionless face. The Japanese soldier was eighteen or nineteen years old.

'Water? Is there any water?' Li asked him.

The Japanese soldier looked at him as if he were a beast of burden.

Li made a drinking gesture again. Not even a stick of furniture could look more wooden than this Japanese, he thought to himself.

'Water . . . !' another Chinese prisoner chimed in, gesticulating and enunciating the syllables slowly and carefully, as if that way he could make the Japanese understand.

But the Japanese did not make a sound or twitch a muscle.

The cry was taken up by a number of the prisoners: 'Water! Water! Water! . . .'

'Why's he being such a bastard? He must know what we're saying! Even if there's no food, just give us a little water!'

'Water! Water!' More and more prisoners were demanding water.

The Japanese officer shouted an order and his men cocked their rifles.

The Chinese soldiers began to mutter things like:

'I knew we shouldn't have come into this ruin. We can't take them on, there's no room to move!'

'If we were going to take them on, we should have done it this morning, before we got so hungry!'

'We could have taken them on last night – there are so many of us and we all had guns!'

'If we'd known how few Japanese there were, we wouldn't have taken any notice of the leaflets. We would have taken them on for sure!'

'Well, we didn't. There's no fucking point in regretting it now,' said Sergeant Major Li.

At this point, the interpreter appeared again. 'Chinese officers and men, there are logistical problems with supplies, and we have to ask you to be patient for a little longer. Once you get to the island, there'll be food.'

'Is that for sure?'

'The lieutenant colonel has guaranteed it! He's arranged for the cooks on the island to have steamed bread for all five thousand of you!'

'Steamed bread for all five thousand!' A discussion rumbled among the Chinese prisoners. A definite figure seemed to give the information added credibility.

'How many each?'

'Will there be enough to fill us up?'

'How long is the boat trip?'

'The boats are already waiting for you on the river,' the interpreter went on. 'Please form up in orderly lines ready to march off . . .'

The prisoners summoned every last ounce of strength

and got unsteadily to their feet, a giddy darkness moment-arily swirling before their eyes. There was a sheen of sweat on the foreheads and backs of many of them. As they made their way out of the gate of the ruined factory, the intepreter announced in a relaxed voice: 'Please cooperate with your captors and hold out your wrists to be tied. We're sorry for the inconvenience but this is to maintain order on the boats!'

In the twilight, all the prisoners could see was a forest of bayonets and the wavering light from a few dozen torches in their faces. 'Please don't get the wrong impression,' the collaborator went on. 'This is simply to ensure the operation proceeds without mishap.'

Sergeant Major Li had the impression that the severity of the Japanese and the collaborator's friendliness were at odds with one another but he was too weak to give it much thought after a day of hunger, thirst, anxiety and fear.

After an hour of marching, they could hear the river ahead of them and the moon emerged from behind the clouds. They dropped into single file as they neared the riverbank. By the time the last of the prisoners arrived, the moon hung in the sky, illuminating the scene brightly.

One by one, the prisoners had their hands tied behind their backs. As they stood on the riverbank, they soon began to ask each other: 'Where are the boats? How come we can't see a single one?'

The interpreter was nowhere to be seen so they could only ask and answer each other. 'I expect they'll be here . . . this isn't the pier, they can't dock here . . . the boats must be moored somewhere nearby . . .'

A fine spray blew into the faces of five thousand prisoners of war.

'So what are we doing here?' asked one.

'Waiting for the boats?' said another.

'Didn't they say the boats would be waiting for us?'

'Who said that?'

'That collaborator who does the interpreting.'

'He's an asshole! There's no pier here, so how can the boats dock? They must be moored nearby and they'll come over when we're ready to board.'

'But why don't they let us walk to the pier and get on the boats?'

At this question, they all fell silent. The speaker was a twenty-one-year-old platoon commander of Li's; he had a bit of an education and a good head on his shoulders. Li saw fear in the young man's eyes: he had sized up the situation as soon as he arrived at the riverbank. They were on a horseshoe-shaped beach which opened towards the Yangtze River and was protected by high ground on the other three sides. The track leading down to the beach was very narrow, which was why the Japanese had made them switch from marching two abreast to single file. There was no way that boats capable of carrying so many men could dock here. It was impossible.

The young man pointed out to Li that, up above them, the high ground was densely packed with Japanese soldiers. The moon shone down on their weapons and on the heavy machine guns which had been set up at intervals.

'What's all this about? What are we waiting for?'

No one could answer this question. Some of the prisoners were too weak to stand and sat down. Hunger and thirst had knocked the fight out of them, and they were resigned to their fate.

And there they waited, till the moon had completed its journey from one side of the sky to the other. Still the boats did not come. Their feet were painfully cold, then went completely numb. Their bound wrists also hurt and eventually they could not feel them any more either.

'Hell, I knew we shouldn't have let them tie our wrists!'

'Right, then we could have fought back!'

'Wasn't their commanding officer's name on the leaflet?'

'How much longer have we got to wait? If we don't freeze to death, we'll starve to death!'

Sergeant Major Li kept looking up at the Japanese soldiers massed on the skyline on all three sides. They seemed to be expecting something, and every machine gun seemed to stand in readiness too. Judging by the position of the moon and the stars, it must be around midnight.

Another couple of hours passed and the prisoners were sick of waiting around, with some becoming quite frantic. The wounded sat leaning against each other, some sharing a padded coat or a quilt between them, moaning and groaning. The cold at that time of night was bone-chilling even for those who had survived unscathed, let alone those with gaping wounds. Only one of the wounded was sound asleep – the boy Wang Pusheng. He, like the other injured men, had gained by not having his wrists tied.

There were half a dozen other men, just then, between Sergeant Major Li and the boy.

Li looked around once more at the Japanese lining the high ground and saw that the sky behind them was beginning to lighten, turning the mass of steel helmets from black to grey. He had just looked back towards the river when he heard a slight sound, so faint he was not sure if he had heard it at all. Something like the sound made by the Japanese officer as he signalled his orders, bringing his sabre down, slicing it cleanly and smoothly through the air.

Li was an intelligent and seasoned old soldier. He knew how to fight and kill, and how to make good his escape and hide. It was the last two skills in particular which had ensured he was still alive and kicking after all these years as a soldier.

So when his ears caught this faint sound, he understood in a flash what it meant and was the first to fling himself to the ground. In the depths of his cynical old soldier's heart, with its distrust of everyone, in particular the enemy, he was aware that he and his five thousand fellow soldiers had walked right into a trap set by the Japanese. Just why they had set that trap he could only guess, but he knew that it had snapped shut on them and no good could come of it.

As soon as he heard the sound he instantly scanned the ground around him. The water's edge was thirty or forty feet away so he could not hope for salvation there. To his right, he saw a slight depression in the ground.

Just then, all the prisoners heard the sound of metal rubbing on metal. 'What's going on?' someone asked.

The simultaneous firing of a dozen machine guns was their answer.

Li dived straight into the depression which his eyes had just alighted on.

A body thudded down on top of him and twitched, the head dangling over him and soaking him in blood and brain matter. Another body rolled first one way then the other, finally landing in the same depression. Li felt as if his abdomen was being crushed. It was incredible how the dying fought to survive. The bodies pressing down on him kept rearing upwards, pain forcing their backs into the sort of arc that only the most skilled acrobat could perform. But with every spasm, the arc grew less pronounced, until the bodies flattened out and the rippling movements ceased. Li learned that people's innards could protest too – the innards of the arcing bodies were emitting brutal and appalling sounds.

The firing went on for a long time, and the corpses covering Sergeant Major Li were shot, quite gratuitously, over and over again. Every time a bullet scored a hit, life would return to a corpse which was growing cold and it would be shaken by a great tremor which went right through Li's body and into his soul. The bullets seemed to be scoring a hit on him too.

When silence had fallen around them and the blood and other fluids from the comrades whose bodies lay on top of him had congealed and gone icy cold, the Japanese came down from the skyline. They tried to clear a path through the corpses which littered the ground but it was not easy so they simply trod roughshod over them. They were grumbling about something, perhaps that the mixture of blood and mud was ruining their boots. As they walked they used their bayonets and the tips of their boots to shove the bodies aside, those bodies who as recently as yesterday thought they were coming here to eat steamed bread and tinned food! These honest Chinese peasants were easily fooled. They had walked right into the trap. The Japanese soldiers yawned and chatted and jabbed their bayonets into any of the bodies which showed any sign of life. Li listened to them chatting and jabbing, making their way in his direction.

Li felt a clammy breeze from the river brush his leg. He hoped the Japanese would ignore it and take it for a dead leg. A few minutes later, his exposed leg was spotted by a Japanese soldier and a bayonet was thrust deep into the sturdy muscles of his thigh. The natural reaction of the flesh was to retract, making it hard to pull the bayonet out. Li bit down ferociously on his lip and willed his leg to seem as insensitive as that of a lifeless corpse. The slightest movement would invite a second shooting and ruin all his efforts to survive. The second stab came, a little below the first. The steel blade pierced the skin and flesh and Li heard it scrape the bone. It was as if his whole body was a sound box, amplifying the sound of the stab in his own ears. He heard the sound of steel grating against flesh as a loud swish. At that instant, every part of his consciousness was erased, and his head was consumed in white light. At the fourth blow of the bayonet, Li felt something snap at the back of his knee, something which ricocheted down to his calf and up to his thigh. At this, the white light in his head enveloped his whole body.

It was the absolute silence which awoke him. He had no idea how long he had been unconscious, but he knew he was still alive. His hunger and thirst had gone, and his body was filled with a white-hot energy, as if it had been reborn.

He waited and waited. Finally, when it started to grow dark, he slowly shifted his position under the pile of corpses and tried to turn over. It should have been impossible. Not even the best military training could have taught any soldier to perform that movement. His hands were tied behind his back and one leg was useless. His other leg had to take his entire weight as he turned.

It must have taken him an hour to move from his prone position to lying on his side. Now it was easier, as he could use one shoulder and one leg together to get into a crawling position. He was very careful to keep his movements to the minimum, as he was not sure that all the Japanese had left the killing grounds. It was getting darker and darker and the pain as he inched forward grew worse. He kept stopping to wipe the sweat from his eyes. By nightfall he had progressed five or six metres, a kind of forced march which left him soaked in sweat, even though he was dehydrated after two days without water. He thought he would crawl towards the river. He had to slake his thirst at all costs. Then he could plan his next movements.

Just then he stopped, the sweat chilling on his skin, because he had heard a faint noise. Could the Japanese have left someone to guard the corpses? He dared not pant, and muffled his gasps by pressing his open mouth against his shoulder. He listened again. The voice spoke Chinese. 'Wounded soldier . . . name of Wang Pusheng . . .'

Li kept looking around but could see no one that looked as if they were alive. He held his breath and froze. The voice came again. '. . . Help me . . .'

He could hear it was a boy. Many young boys had been

snatched by press gangs recently. The boy must have thought his wheezing cry was a loud call for help which could be heard for miles around.

When Li found him, Wang Pusheng was buried under a pile of corpses, as he himself had been. He had been bayoneted in the belly but had been partly shielded by a corpse whose lower leg lay across him. Otherwise the wound would have been much bigger. The corners of Wang Pusheng's mouth pulled at the bandage which covered most of his face. Li could tell that the boy was in terrible pain and wanted to cry but had no tears left. 'No crying!' he threatened him. 'If you cry I won't take you with me! Just remember how incredibly lucky you are to have survived!'

The boy soldier pressed his lips together. Li held out his bound hands to the boy and told him to undo the rope. The boy set to work feebly. It took more than an hour, during which time both of them gave up several times, but finally Li's hands were freed. It was now much easier for Li to move three out of his four limbs. He crawled down to the water's edge. He had to push some of his comrades' corpses into the water in order to reach it. He drank a bellyful of river water foul with blood, then soaked an army cap and crawled back with it to Wang Pusheng, squeezing the drops out for the boy. The boy gripped the cap as if it were his mother's breast and pressed it into his open mouth.

When they had drunk enough, they lay side by side and smoked a pipe. Li still had his pipe on him, and went through the pockets of nearby corpses until he found a pipe for Wang Pusheng.

'We've had something to drink and now a smoke, my lad, and that'll get us going,' said Li. 'Now we're going to make a break for it.'

The boy had never imagined he would smoke his very first pipe in the middle of a pile of corpses. He copied Sergeant Major Li, breathing in the smoke and exhaling. He hoped the sergeant was telling the truth and smoking really would get him going.

'If someone has no water, they'll die in three days. With water you can live for a lot longer,' the sergeant major went on.

It took them a long time to finish their pipes. By that time, Li knew that he could not abandon Wang Pusheng. But he still had no idea how he was going to make his escape carrying a soldier whose guts were spilling out, when one of his own legs was out of action. While he had been smoking, he had considered their options. High ground hemmed in the shore on three sides, and only one slope looked possible to climb. The Japanese had chosen this particular patch of riverbank as an execution ground with great care. It had one more advantage: to dispose of the corpses they only had to push them into the water, and the river would carry them away.

Li found a first-aid kit in the pocket of a dead company commander. He tore it open and extracted bandages and swabs. There was a tube in the bag as well; and Li guessed it must be an antiseptic cream. He covered a swab with it and pushed the swab into the cavity in Wang Pusheng's abdomen. The boy howled with pain.

'Look at the sky, our planes are coming!' said Li.

Wang Pusheng looked up at the night sky through tear-drenched eyes and Li quickly poked back in a piece of intestine which was spilling out.

Wang Pusheng did not make a sound this time. Instead he fainted.

It was lucky Wang Pusheng had not eaten in two or three days and his gut was completely empty, Li thought. That meant there would be less danger of infection. He waited for him to regain consciousness before he carried him away.

If by any chance the boy did not come to, then Li would go alone.

Wang Pusheng's breathing was shallow and ragged. Several times, Li could not feel any warmth on the finger that he held over the boy's mouth. But he felt his chest carefully and discovered his heart was still beating.

Li knew that the longer they waited, the fewer their chances of escape. The enemy would be back eventually to deal with the corpses, perhaps by daybreak. But the boy soldier would not wake up. Li realised his fists were tightly clenched, not from the pain in his leg but from the anguish of having to wait.

Li may have been in two minds as to whether he should leave this boy behind and make good his own escape. But when he was telling this part of the story to Major Dai, he did not acknowledge it. Instead, he said that he really could not be so immoral as to abandon the seriously wounded boy, because, after all, Wang Pusheng had undone his wrists for him. He watched over Wang Pusheng all night until the sky began to lighten.

At dawn, Wang Pusheng regained consciousness. Bright, dark eyes opened in a face as ashen as a corpse. He looked at Sergeant Major Li lying beside him, both of them sharing a greatcoat which was stiff with blood. 'We'd better go, my lad,' said Li.

The boy said something, but so faintly that Li could not hear.

'What?'

The boy repeated it and Li understood this time: he could not walk and would rather be left here to die. He could not bear any more pain like that.

'You mean, you've made me waste all night waiting for you?!' said Li.

'Wait a bit longer till my belly stops hurting,' Wang begged him, 'then I'll go with you.'

Li watched as the sky grew lighter. Then he draped the boy's arm over his shoulder. He was a well-trained soldier, after all, and could drag himself along on one leg even with someone slung over his shoulder. One good thing was that the boy weighed no more than a shoulder-pole of grain.

The mist rose from the river and would give them some cover. That was another good thing, a very good thing.

They had only moved a few feet when they heard the sound of footsteps. Li's heart was in his mouth, but they were both still hidden by the mist and he could squeeze them in between two corpses.

The footsteps were coming from the hilltop, but did not sound like army boots. Then came the words: 'There must be thousands of them here!'

They were speaking Chinese!

'We haven't seen them all yet. It's still misty. Those fuckers, to kill so many Chinese soldiers!'

'Fucking Jap devils!'

The men were talking Nanking dialect and must have been in their forties or fifties.

'There are only a few of us. How long is it going to take to get rid of all these corpses?!'

'Fucking Jap devils!'

Down the slope they came, cursing and complaining.

'They'll clog up the river if we throw them in!'

'Hurry up, otherwise those fuckers'll be after us!'

The men, ant-like amid this scene of devastation, got to work.

Li reckoned it would be best to show themselves now, without waiting any longer. The Japanese might be here any moment. Even if the Chinese men were willing to help them, they could not do it under the noses of the Japanese.

'Brothers, please help us!' he shouted.

In an instant, the men's chatter stopped and silence fell.

It was so quiet that they could hear the loud slapping of waves against the corpses in the water.

'Help us! . . .'

One man made his way towards them, planting his feet carefully in the cracks between shoulders, heads, legs and arms.

'We're here!' Li shouted, to guide the man through the mist.

Emboldened, the other men followed, threading their way through the mountains of bodies until they reached Sergeant Major Li and Wang Pusheng. As one, their arms went down and Li and Wang were lifted up and carried up the slope to the top.

'Don't make any noise!' ordered the man carrying Li. 'We'll find a place to hide you and then figure out what to do when it gets dark again.'

Li found out that the little group all dressed in black waistcoats had been commandeered by the Japanese as labourers. Their task was to dispose of the Chinese prisoners who had been secretly executed.

Nine

When, three hours after Fabio had sent Ah Gu to look for the pond, he still wasn't back, Fabio could stand it no more. He went down to the cellar and asked Yumo whether she had given Ah Gu clear directions to the pond. Yes she had, she said, and in fact Ah Gu said he knew it: it was in the grounds of a clan memorial hall, and the family used it in summer to grow lotuses.

'He's been gone more than three hours!' exclaimed Fabio.

He changed into the newer of his two cassocks and gave his face a wipe with a towel. If he was to rescue Ah Gu from the Japanese, he needed to have an air of authority about him. He had to find Ah Gu. Without him, there was no one to carry water. George Chen could not go – the Japanese would definitely round up a young man like him.

Fabio headed north along the narrow street which passed their entrance, according to Yumo's instructions. When he reached the second alleyway, he turned into it and walked right down to the end. It all looked different from the last time he had come this way: the walls were blackened and some buildings had disappeared. Half a dozen dogs scrabbled out of his way as he passed. The dogs had grown fat in the last few days and their coats gleamed. Fabio averted his gaze whenever he saw a pack of curs gathered around something.

He was carrying a tin bucket in his right hand and was prepared to hurl it at the dogs to fend them off if necessary. Once they had gorged on human flesh, they might switch to eating the living too. As he emerged from the alley, he saw an old wall of hard-fired, grey bricks in front of him. Through a gap where it had collapsed, he could see a pond glittering in the morning light. There was no sign of Ah Gu. Fabio realised he would have to give up his search.

The surface of the pond was covered in lotus leaves. It was the most peaceful scene Fabio had seen in a long time. He drew a bucketful of water from the pond and took the same way back to the church. It was a piffling amount now that they had so many people to look after. Father Engelmann's beloved old Ford would have to be pressed into use to fetch more.

Back at the church, Fabio pulled out the Ford's back seats and loaded it up with every bucket, bowl and pot the church possessed. Then he and George drove off to the pond. When they arrived back after the first trip, George used the water to make a pot of rice porridge. Everyone got a bowlful, and a little dish of pickled vegetables which smelled like old rags and tasted foul, although they all said they were delicious.

Fabio looked on as the women and girls washed themselves. None of them had washed in days. Today they each got a cup of water and, clustered around the gutter under the eaves, they dipped their handkerchiefs into it and wiped their faces. Then they used what remained to rinse their mouths and clean their teeth.

Yumo wet her hair ribbon and carefully rubbed behind her ears and around the back of her neck. Her handkerchief would use up too much of the precious water. Then she undid her top buttons, wrung out the green ribbon and reached in to wipe the upper part of her chest. She looked up, to see Fabio standing staring at her. He looked away in shame but he couldn't deny that he had feelings growing for her which seemed to reach blindly towards the light like a vine twisting out from under a stone.

* * *

It was even colder that night. As the gunshots outside the compound went on incessantly, powdery snow fell in the windless dark. It was as if the snow were shaken out of the atmosphere by the gunshots. The air was damp. It was the kind of snow that would make everything dirty the next day.

As the schoolgirls were filing back to the attic after evening prayers, they heard the faint sound of singing coming from the cellar. Up in the attic Shujuan longed to ask Xiaoyu to sneak down with her to see what was going on, but they were no longer speaking to each other. Since Xiaoyu had betrayed her, Shujuan had not tried to make it up with her, and made a point of turning her back to her in bed. Xiaoyu was never short of close friends, however, and Anna had immediately taken Shujuan's place.

Shujuan waited until the girls were snoring and then crept downstairs. Outside, the cold air was biting. She huddled in the snow and peered down into the cellar. At first all she could see was the back of a broad-shouldered, slender-waisted man. In spite of the long, baggy woollen garment he wore, he looked every inch the soldier, the sort who would turn any garment into a military uniform. Shujuan knew that this was the officer who had almost succeeded in pushing the Japanese Army right into the Huangpu River. He had told Father Engelmann all about it. Major Dai was livid about the retreat from Shanghai and the abandonment of Nanking. He could not understand it. If the great retreat ordered by the Nationalist military command had been intended to save lives and to conserve military strength, then why had Chiang Kai-shek turned down a three-day truce between the Japanese and the Chinese which had been negotiated by the International Safety Committee, and would have permitted an orderly retreat from Nanking and a peaceful handover of the city to the Japanese?

The prostitutes had dressed the young soldier Wang Pusheng in Hongling's mink coat. They did not have enough bandages and were using patterned silk scarves instead. Wang was a delicate boy to start with; now he almost looked like a girl. He sat up in a makeshift bed, with Cardamom next to him. They had playing cards in their hands and a sheet of newspaper between them served as a card table.

Shujuan had a restricted view down through the ventilation grille, and could only see whoever happened to come into the frame. Now it was Zhao Yumo; Shujuan could see her talking to the major in low tones, too low for Shujuan to catch what they were saying, no matter how hard she strained to hear. The major appeared to be getting amorous with this Yumo.

Shujuan felt a surge of hatred for these prostitutes. If they had not forced their way in, the water in the cistern would have been enough for the sixteen girls. The women had used up all the water washing their clothes, their faces and their bums, and made the schoolgirls drink from a filthy pond. In fact, if they had not run out of water, Ah Gu would not have needed to leave the compound, and would not now be missing. Even the heroic Major Dai was letting them have their way with him, right now, before her very eyes. He had let down his defences. He had become dissolute.

Driven by her fury, Shujuan went to the ash pit behind the kitchen and collected a shovelful of coal dust in which a few embers still glowed. She went back to the ventilation shaft and weighed the shovel speculatively in her hand: if she could get half of it down the shaft and a couple of sparks fell on the faces of those sluts who fed off men's weaknesses, how happy she would be! How good it would make her and her classmates feel!

*   *   *

Down in the cellar, Zhao Yumo sat to one side on an overturned wine barrel and smoked a cigarette while the other women played poker and mah-jong. Major Dai sat beside her.

'The first time I set eyes on you here, you looked familiar,' he said.

Yumo smiled. 'Surely not! I mean, you're not from Nanking.'

'Nor are you! Have you lived in Shanghai?'

'Yes. I was born in Suzhou and I spent seven or eight years in Shanghai.'

'Have you been to Shanghai recently?'

'Several times.'

'Who with? With a soldier? This July?'

'The end of July. Just when it was at its hottest.'

'You must have gone to the Air Fleet Club. I often go there myself.'

'How would I remember?' said Yumo, although her smile seemed to indicate that she remembered perfectly well; she just did not want to admit it because she guarded the discretion of all her clients.

A yell from Hongling interrupted their conversation.

'But I can't dance! We're all country bumpkins! Yumo's the only one who's been to all the clubs in Shanghai. She dances really well.'

Sergeant Major Li had been asking Hongling to dance for him, and this was her response.

All the women agreed with Hongling.

'Yumo can charm statues of the Bodhisattva into life when she dances!' one chimed in.

'Miss Zhao, your soldier brothers risk their lives constantly . . . if we ask you to dance for us, should you not do us the honour?' said Major Dai.

'Right!' agreed Hongling. 'Live for the day! The Japanese might be here tonight, then there'll be no tomorrow for us!'

Sergeant Major Li seemed to feel his rank was too humble for him to address Yumo directly and muttered something to Hongling. Then he grinned broadly as Hongling cajoled her leader on his behalf.

'Who's not heard of the fairy-tale palace in Nanking

where Zhao Yumo hides out? It's always full of fine men feasting their eyes on her!'

'Well, I suppose, when we get old and long in the tooth, we won't be able to wriggle our hips any more!' said Yumo, getting to her feet.

Yumo's neat, rounded buttocks undulated in a rumba. She fixed her gaze on Major Dai, and a response appeared in his eyes. But he could not keep it up for long and, with a young man's shyness, he dropped his eyes and conceded defeat. But Yumo, the seductress, kept enticing him back to her. She wore a purple velvet cheongsam, against which her face, untouched by the sun, gleamed palely. She had certainly earned her place at the top of her profession: she carried herself easily, like a cultured, elegant, society lady. It was only these flashing looks that gave men a taste of the coquette under the surface.

There was a strict hierarchy in the Nanking brothels, and each grade was awarded a different salary. The Qin Huai women wore insignia on their clothes when they were at work, indicating their status. That way the clients could weigh out the family silver in advance, and work out who they could afford to enjoy that day. The people of Nanking had never been overly concerned about the morality of prostitution; in fact, generations of literati had sung the praises of prostitutes – from the Eight Beauties of Qin Huai to Sai Jinhua who rose to become wife of a diplomat – and had given them positive roles in their writings.

Yumo, who at work wore a five-star insignia, was standing in front of Sergeant Major Li now. He was a simple sort of a fellow and found it agonising to have this woman right in front of him without being able to get his hands on her. All he could do was smile foolishly. Even Wang Pusheng, just a slip of a boy, was enthralled by Yumo's dancing. Only Cardamom was still absorbed in her poker game.

'Your go!' Cardamom turned to look at the boy. His small face swathed in multicoloured bandages, he was staring goggle-eyed at Yumo's torso and belly, and she gave him a slap.

The evening the gravedigger brought Sergeant Major Li and Wang Pusheng to the church, Cardamom had given up her bed to Wang Pusheng. She first cleaned and dressed the wound in his abdomen and found the gaping hole, an inch and a half wide, in the paper-thin skin. It pouted like a pair of lips drooling red saliva and something grey and soft poked out of it. Sergeant Major Li told the women that when he poked back the intestines, he had tried to get it all back in, but a bit got left on the outside. However, there was nothing to be done until Fabio Adornato or Father Engelmann could get a doctor from the Safety Zone to come. Cardamom promptly became Wang Pusheng's nurse, doing everything for him, from giving him food and water to washing him.

Cardamom's slap brought Wang Pusheng to his senses, and he smiled at her. Cardamom was smitten. They were about the same age and both separated from their families. She knew nothing about hers, not even her own surname. She had been kidnapped by an itinerant busker from north of the Huai River and sold into the brothel.

Cardamom was then an exquisitely pretty but lazy, peevish and unambitious seven-year-old who could not even be bothered with learning to do her hair properly. She complained she had been cheated if she lost at cards, and insisted on the winnings if she won. A year passed, and her clients were mainly foot-runners, cooks and common soldiers. After five years of beatings, she managed to learn how to play the *pipa* but she still dressed in the other girls' hand-me-downs, all patched and ill-fitting. The brothel madam used to say to her: 'Cardamom, all you can do is eat!' Cardamom took the comment in good part, and agreed: 'Yes, that's right!' The only thing she had going for her was that if a man took a liking to her, she would put heart and soul into attending on him.

With someone she was keen on, she would exclaim: 'You're a fellow countryman!' so the world was full of Cardamom's fellow countrymen. If she wanted to cadge a gift from a client or the other women, she would say: 'Ai-ya! I'd completely forgotten, today's my birthday!'

Now she asked Wang Pusheng: 'Why d'you keep watching her?'

'I don't,' said the boy.

'When you're better, I'll take you to a really big dance hall,' said Cardamom.

'But I might die tomorrow,' objected Wang Pusheng.

Cardamom clapped her hand over his mouth, spat, and scuffed the spit into the floor with her foot. 'Less of that nonsense! If you die then I'm going with you!'

She was overheard by Hongling, who shouted over: 'Amazing! Listen to those two lovebirds!'

Wang Pusheng flushed scarlet and his mouth opened so wide the corners disappeared into the enveloping bandages.

'Leave him alone,' said Cardamom. 'He's only a boy!'

The women laughed. They thought it very funny when Cardamom played 'big sister'.

'And how do you know he's a boy, Cardamom?' teased Sergeant Major Li.

Only Yumo, still carried away with her dancing, paid no attention; she was so wildly flushed that her cheeks looked as though they were painted. Although, to the others, it seemed that she thought only of the movements of her body, her mind was far away. She was remembering a man she met in a dance hall. A man who had filled her with hopes, which he then shattered.

His name was Zhang Shitiao. His family had been merchants for many generations, but when he was born, his grandfather decided to make this eldest grandson a scholar. The boy first studied abroad and then returned to become section head at the Ministry of Education in Nanking. This was just the sort of step up in the world the family wanted him to make and was the reason why they had invested so much money in his education. He made a good marriage and lived an upright life. And so it would have continued if he had not spent an evening visiting the Sina Dance Hall with his former classmates. It was his chance meeting with Zhao Yumo that night which led him into the dissolute life he began to lead. If it had been a woman like Hongling or Cardamom, he would not even have exchanged a word with her. But then, women like Hongling and Cardamom could not go to that kind of a dance hall. The Sina Dance Hall on Central Road was a small and exclusive establishment. The very best lady singers and dancers were performing in the show, *Kabbalah*, that night and tickets were one silver dollar each. Sometimes the most popular dancers would only agree to dance if they were paid three or four dollars. It was the kind of place frequented by young men and women from rich families, but only behind their parents' backs.

That evening was Yumo's lucky break. She was looking extremely elegant, wearing a string of pearls which were obviously genuine, and holding a copy of the *Modern Magazine*. From her get-up she looked like an unmarried girl from a rich family, although with a slightly aloof air which gave the impression of unusual maturity. As Shitiao's party entered the dance hall, they spotted the young woman sitting in one of the armchairs which lined the sides. She was just the sort of girl they were looking for. One of Shitiao's friends thought she might be waiting for a girlfriend, another that she had danced until her shoes hurt her and was giving her feet a rest. Shitiao watched as two of his friends went up and asked her to dance and were rebuffed with a tactful smile. Then they picked on him and told him to try his luck.

Shitiao asked her if she would do him the honour of taking a cup of coffee with him. She looked at him shyly but stood up and waited as he helped her on with her coat, just like any young lady used to Western manners. Behind them, Shitiao could hear his friends wolf-whistling above the music, presumably because they were jealous.

'What's your name?' he asked politely.

'Zhao Yumo. And yours, sir?'

What a self-possessed young woman, he thought as he answered her question. They drank their coffee, and he asked what she was studying. She showed him what she had been reading. The *Modern Magazine* had articles on just about anything current: politics, economics, lifestyle and health, and the scandalous things which film stars were getting up to. There was more to her than dignified elegance, Shitiao felt. From time to time, she would shoot radiant glances in his direction until he was covered with a sheen of sweat, his throat tightening and his heart swelling in his chest. This was a woman whose femininity (and she was supremely feminine) was just waiting to be released. Traditionally, a man set up a family with a decent woman like his mother, yet that deprived him of so much, emotionally and physically. Any man with a bit of experience of life understood that no matter how womanly and coquettish a girl, marriage would instantly kill her desire for pleasure. A girl who combined the attractions of a prostitute with a respectable family background was an impossibility. But the other way round, outwardly a lady but a whore in your bed, that was possible. Someone like Zhao Yumo, for example.

Yumo was a highly ambitious and resourceful woman. She could adapt her language and behaviour to people from all walks of life. She had always thought she had been born into the wrong family – she should have been the petted daughter of wealthy parents. She was worth just as much as any of them. She had been well educated in the classics, played the *pipa* and could paint and do calligraphy. Her parents were people of status and education but hopeless with money and, at the age of ten, she had been given by her father to an uncle to pay off a gambling debt. After the man died, his widow sold her to a brothel on the Qin Huai River. By the age of fourteen, she knew all the tricks of the trade. When she played drinking games, she could quote lines from classical poetry and even knew all about the allusions in the poems. She was twenty-four when Shitiao met her, and she had made up her mind that she would not tell him she was a prostitute; she would wait until he was so smitten by her that he was ready to abandon his family for her. At her age, she had to start looking for a different kind of life. She could not go on drinking with clients for ever.

She began to tell Shitiao about her life one day in a hotel bedroom. By now, Shitiao was feeling that it was wonderful to be a man and that, in fact, he had wasted the previous thirty years of his life. His ideal woman lay beside him. He did not yet know that Yumo really was a dyed-in-the-wool, grade-one professional prostitute.

She told him half-truths about herself: how she was a virgin until the age of nineteen and had only kept the men company as they drank, and danced for them. One day she met a man and, when he said he wanted to marry her, gave herself to him. When this heartless man broke off their engagement and left her after a couple of years, she was broken-hearted. She fell so gravely ill she almost died. She nestled in Shitiao's arms, weeping as she told him the sad tale. Even the most hard-bitten man would not have doubted her words, let alone a young man like Zhang Shitiao, ready to right all wrongs and with a heart as soft as glutinous rice.

Not only was he not disgusted by Yumo's outpourings, he swore on his life that he would not be the second man in her life to let her down.

It was Shitiao's wife who revealed the truth about Yumo to her husband. She found a hotel manager's name card in his suit pocket and racked her brains as to why her husband should have been staying in a hotel. One thing they did not lack at home was rooms. He could only have gone to the hotel for some nefarious reason. She called the number on the card and asked the manager: 'Is Mr Zhang Shitiao there?' The manager addressed her as Miss Zhao. Shitiao's wife was a resourceful woman and pretended to be 'Miss Zhao'. 'Mr Zhang said to tell you,' the manager went on, 'that he'll be there today at four o'clock, an hour late, and please will you wait for him.'

It only took Mr Zhang's wife half a day to dig up the dirt on Zhao Yumo. Then she presented her husband with the facts. He categorically denied that Yumo was a prostitute until she mobilised all his old school friends and he was forced to face the fact that there was only one Zhao Yumo in Nanking and that was the famed prostitute of the Qin Huai brothel. However, it was too late. By then, Yumo's emotional and sexual arts had ensnared him. He insisted that she was the most beautiful and most unfortunate woman in the world. According to him, his friends and family only despised her because they were all of the intellectual class!

In the event, though, it did not prove too difficult to turn Shitiao from his wicked ways. His wife only had to put on a tragic face, accept the painful truth that she had been wronged, and throw herself into caring for his family. Shitiao had spent six years in Europe. He prided himself on his humanist spirit. He never wanted to hurt anyone, let alone someone who was weak, especially when they had already been wronged. His wife not only endured her sufferings silently; she was also suffering from both pretended and real sicknesses. She looked miserable and her breathing grew weak, but she forbore to lay a single word of blame at his door. She never even asked him where he went every evening. Shitiao's sympathies gradually shifted over to his wife's side. He bickered with Yumo when they met and began to find her little ways and moods less appealing. When all government departments made the wartime move from Nanking to Chongqing, he at first said he would buy Yumo's freedom from the brothel and would get her boat ticket so that she could quietly follow the family to Chongqing. But the day before they were due to leave, he sent her a letter saying he had been wounded in an air raid and would have to postpone the transfer to Chongqing. For the moment, he would be going with his wife to Huizhou, her home city, to convalesce in peaceful country surroundings. With the letter he enclosed fifty silver dollars and a gold bar, a gift which was less generous than that of her former lover, who had left her with a diamond ring. To Zhang, a senior civil servant in the Ministry for Education, who believed that everyone was born equal, Yumo was worth only one gold bar and fifty silver dollars.

'Shameless bitches!'

Yumo's reverie was broken by a shout that came down the ventilation shaft.

'Who's up there?' asked Yumo.

'Stinking bitches!' came the same voice.

The women looked at each other. It was one of the schoolgirls.

'You wait until the Japs make you into a bitch!' Hongling shouted back. 'You think you're better than us, but when they pull your trousers down, you're just the same!'

Nani joined in.

'Don't you know the Japs love making whores out of nice young girls?'

'The Japs have searched the Safety Zone and taken dozens of young girls away!' Hongling gloated cheerfully.

*   *   *

Up above the cellar, as she sat with her shovelful of embers waiting to strike, Shujuan shuddered. Her shoulders were covered with snow but it was the women's words that caused her to shake. Was it true what that bitch Nani said? It couldn't be. She was just trying to frighten her.

Shujuan was measuring the length of the shovel, estimating how to aim it to get the most devastating results with the live embers, when she heard a voice behind her.

'What are you doing?'

Ash and shovel dropped to the ground, and Shujuan turned to find Deacon Adornato looming over her. He looked at the ash with its glowing sparks and repeated his question. 'What are you doing?'

Shujuan said nothing, just jumped up and pressed herself against the wall. She could not have stood more rigid if she had been put in the corner by her teacher. Fabio was a tall man and could not see the 'peep show' going on at the bottom of the shaft.

The cellar grew rowdier; there was clapping and the tempo of the dance quickened.

Telling Shujuan to go back to bed, Fabio went towards the kitchen door. Shujuan leaned over the shaft to watch what would happen.

Yumo had thrown off her high-society airs and graces and was dancing a different dance now, the jitterbug. This was even more seductive. As she undulated, she bumped Major Dai with her shoulder or her crotch. The major was transfixed, leering like an old soldier. Yumo dropped all pretence at coyness and became completely brazen. She knew full well that the schoolgirl was still watching her, and she was aiming to show her that she was not just a 'bitch' but acknowledged as 'top bitch'.

Shujuan saw the women pause for a moment and look up. She knew they must have heard Fabio shout down: 'Open the trapdoor!'

After a fractional hesitation, Yumo resumed her dance.

Someone must have opened the trapdoor because now Fabio was in the cellar.

Yumo flashed a smile at him.

'Quiet!' Fabio commanded in English.

Hongling did not understand. 'Yangzhou Fabio's come!'

she said. 'Dance a dance with me and keep me warm, Yangzhou Fabio!'

Fabio's tone of voice was different from when he spoke in Chinese. He said again in accented English: 'Please stop.' He looked drawn and haggard, and his face was devoid of all emotion. He had assumed an air of lofty spirituality, as if he were looking down from on high on a bunch of maggots.

It had its effect: faced with this silent, expressionless clergyman, the women quieted down. Yumo pulled out a cigarette, somewhat bent from her dancing, lit it from the candle and took a long in-breath. Major Dai went up to her and lit a cigarette for himself from hers.

'Please remember that this is not a Qin Huai brothel!' said Fabio.

'So you know just what our brothels look like, do you, Father?' Nani continued to tease him impudently.

'Have you been inside one?' asked Jade with a lewd cackle.

All the women laughed.

Fabio shot Yumo a glance which said: *I always knew your air of refinement was humbug. Now you've shown what you're really made of. Fine, just don't ever play the grande dame with me again, and don't try working your charms on me either.*

'I'm sorry, Father. Everyone's really been feeling the cold and they drank some wine and had a dance to warm up a bit,' Major Dai explained with dignity.

'That's all very well,' said Fabio, 'but you women shouldn't give people an excuse to call you "singing girls heedless that national calamity looms . . .".'

Yumo stared at him with her large dark eyes.

Hongling finished the poem for him: '". . . As, on the far bank, they sing the lament *Courtyard Blooms*."'

'Hongling's not just a pretty face!' one of the other prostitutes shouted mockingly. 'She's got classical poetry in her belly as well as wheat bran!'

'It's the only two lines of poetry I know,' Hongling smiled. 'When our clients abuse us, we quote poetry at them. It's the best way to deal with a scolding.'

'I can't,' said Nani, 'and nor can Cardamom. I bet if you abuse her, she'll play the *pipa* for you!'

'I'll *pipa* you!' retorted Cardamom.

'If you could see what Nanking was like now with your own eyes, its population decreasing every second of every day, you wouldn't behave so disgracefully,' said Fabio.

Shujuan smiled in triumph as she saw the whore Yumo hang her head.

Ten

When Fabio drove to collect water from the pond the next day, Ah Gu's body emerged from the mud. Fabio's stomach churned as he tried to imagine how the old servant had died. He pictured him at the pond with two buckets strung from his shoulder-pole. He must have bumped into Japanese soldiers who, no doubt, demanded the buckets. Ah Gu would not have understood what they said and the Japanese probably found it less trouble to shoot at him than to explain. Ah Gu must have panicked and tried to run but ended up in the pond. Perhaps then a second bullet hit him and he sank beneath the water.

Fabio waded knee-deep in the mud and pulled Ah Gu

towards the bank. As he heaved and heaved, he sensed he had an audience: behind him stood a dozen Japanese, their guns trained on him. But when Fabio turned round, the guns were lowered one by one. As a white man, he got better treatment than Ah Gu.

Fabio drove back with the body. Ah Gu had been thin and dark-skinned. Now his corpse was bloated and bleached pale from immersion in the pond water. Father Engelmann gave the old servant a simple funeral and he was buried in the graveyard behind the church.

After George had shovelled the last earth into the grave and gone back to the kitchen with Fabio, Father Engelmann stayed in the graveyard. The cypresses stood dense with their second growth. They were mighty good cypresses; good enough to build another Noah's Ark. It was a windless morning, yet the treetops stirred nervously. He knelt down beside Ah Gu's grave and his knees crackled like charcoal in a fire. Several days with insufficient food had altered the way he moved, made him slower. He risked feeling faint if he did not give his blood enough time to pump to his head. Recently he had been economising on movements, reducing them to the absolutely necessary minimum, so that no calories should go to waste.

It was eerily quiet. Under the austere tombstones lay missionaries from America from over one hundred years ago. One grave that stood out from the rest belonged to the church's founder, Father Roesing. It looked elaborate but incomplete. Several months ago, a severe rainstorm had flooded the graveyard, which was lower than the rest of the church compound, and Father Roesing's grave had collapsed. In the middle of reconstruction, the workers went to join the refugees fleeing the war, leaving the job unfinished. Now, the fallen cross lay on the ground.

Despite the fact that the church compound was more crowded than it had ever been, Father Engelmann felt entirely alone. He couldn't even talk to Fabio, despite having known him for years. He didn't know why, but he and Fabio always seemed to get off on the wrong foot; whenever Fabio came to talk to him, he was enjoying a bit of peace and quiet, and when he emerged and longed to talk to Fabio, the younger priest was either half-hearted about engaging in conversation or was simply nowhere to be found. Father Engelmann came to the sad conclusion that most people in the world were like himself and Fabio – unable to leave each other alone, but equally unable to be together. When A wanted B, B would be entirely happy with his own company and would not want to be disturbed. And when B needed the companionship or looked for solace in A's company, his needs would just be a burden on A. Untimely demands for companionship were an irritating nuisance. In order to guarantee that one would not have to suffer this nuisance, it was necessary to spurn all human companionship. Human beings came together not because they got on well but because they could not do without each other.

Just now he was having to put up with the companionship of the women and soldiers in the cellar, and it was a nuisance, pure and simple. What was more, it was hugely dangerous.

The day after the gravedigger had left the wounded soldiers at the church, Father Engelmann had made a trip to the Safety Zone. He discovered that the Japanese Army were searching it several times a day, and taking away any fit young men they could find on the pretext that they must be Chinese soldiers in hiding. The authorities rushed madly hither and thither in a futile attempt to get them back. If any young men were so foolish as to offer resistance, they would be shot on the spot. When Father Engelmann heard this, he swallowed back the request he had been about to make – that his colleagues in the Safety Zone take in the wounded soldiers. He did, however, have a quiet word with

Dr Robinson, who was treating an endless stream of injuries; could he spare an hour to come to the church to perform an operation? What kind of operation? asked the doctor. A wound in the abdomen. He had no sooner said these words when Dr Robinson asked him anxiously if this was a Chinese prisoner of war. If so, Engelmann should get rid of him as soon as possible. Some scumbag on the burial team had betrayed the gravediggers who had tried to save the Chinese prisoners, the doctor told him. As a result, early the next morning, the Japanese had buried a number of gravediggers alive. From now on, labourers disposing of the corpses would be under close surveillance. Everyone was under close surveillance. Dr Robinson warned Father Engelmann that the church was by no means safe.

*   *   *

Major Dai watched Father Engelmann kneeling in the grave-yard. He wasn't sure why he had come here, to the place where he had first broken into the church compound. He just knew he couldn't carry on playing mah-jong with the prostitutes. He had to get away, to start being useful. Spending any amount of time with women drove him mad, especially women like these, who kicked up such a fuss about the most trivial thing. He felt thoroughly dejected and confused. He would rather have died cleanly in battle than spend his time with these powdered and painted women. Only one woman understood his grief, and that was Zhao Yumo. If only he could find where Father Engelmann had hidden his gun, he could leave this prison.

Father Engelmann looked up and saw him. 'Good afternoon, Major,' he said. 'Are you looking for something?'

Dai said nothing, suppressing his desire to ask for his pistol back.

It was strange: Father Engelmann's Chinese should have been perfect by now, yet it sounded so foreign. It was as if the Chinese words were giving expression to foreign thought processes and feelings.

Father Engelmann cast a complacent glance around the cemetery. Then he read out the names of the seven priests who lay beneath the tombstones, rather as if he were introducing them at a social gathering. Dai listened patiently, feigning interest.

'Do you think these Westerners are stupid to travel halfway across the world only to end up buried here?' Father Engelmann asked.

Dai wasn't sure how to answer.

Father Engelmann tried another question. 'Where were you trained in the Soviet Union?'

'Moscow.'

'Russia always produces excellent soldiers. Because of their lack of rationality. And Chinese armies fight lousy battles, also for lack of rationality.'

Father Engelmann smiled to himself. He was talking with this Chinese army officer in this manner because his own rationality was wearing thin. Only he himself knew how sensitive and emotional he really was. Usually, if he ever felt this way, he would go and find some friends in the Western community to talk to over a cup of tea. Now they were somewhere in the US or other countries, reading the news about this hell, thanking God they had fled it.

'I have been thinking about this lack of rationality in the East. It gives birth to the most exquisite literature and arts in Russia, Japan and China, yet also the most unthinkable cruelty –'

'Father,' Dai interrupted, 'I want to leave here. I have to . . . I have to go away. I have to leave the other men here with you.'

'To go where?'

'Please return my weapon to me.'

'You won't get far. The Japanese are everywhere. They have three hundred thousand soldiers in Nanking. If you're armed, it'll be even harder to get away.'

'I can't stay here any more,' said Dai. What he had wanted to say, but did not, was that he felt as if he would rot if he had to stay in that cellar any longer.

'Where's your home?' asked the priest.

Dai gave him a strange look. 'Hebei Province,' he replied. His father was an old soldier who bore dozens of scars on his body to prove it. He was almost illiterate, so the only route to promotion for him had been fearlessness in the face of death. Dai and his elder brother had both been to army school, and his sisters had married soldiers. His entire family had dedicated themselves to the service of their country. But he kept his response to the priest to its simplest.

It was as if Father Engelmann could see through him, to the heroism which was in his blood, because his next words were: 'There are so many soldiers whom I despise, the ones whose only thought is to get promotion, make money and grab as many women as they can. But I can see you're different from them.'

'Can you give me my weapon back?'

'Let's talk about that in a minute, shall we?' said Father Engelmann. 'First, tell me, are you married?'

'Uh-huh.' This answer was even briefer than the last.

'Children?'

'One son.' Dai felt a pang as he said this. His son was only five. The journey to adulthood was a long one. Would the boy have his father by his side as he grew up?

'I was only ten when my mother died,' said the priest.

His tone of voice was so poignant that it caught Dai's attention.

'And my father died when I was sixteen.'

'Did you convert to Catholicism after your father died?' asked Dai politely.

'No, my parents were both Roman Catholics,' said Engelmann. 'But I only started studying theology at the age of twenty. At that time I was suffering from a severe bout of depression.'

'Why?'

'I don't know. It just happened.'

Actually this was not true. His depression had been triggered by unrequited love. Since childhood he had been secretly in love with a girl and thought that she felt the same way. However, he finally found out that his feelings were not returned.

'Anyway, I was almost at the point of ending it all when I met an old tramp who was dying from diphtheria. I was living with my brother at the time, and I hid the tramp in the cattle shed behind a heap of fodder. I was in charge of the cattle so no one ever went in there except me. I got medicine for him and took food to him every day. Slowly I nursed him back to health. I got great satisfaction from every small improvement in his condition, more satisfaction than I'd ever had from anything before. It took a whole winter. When he was finally better he thanked me for saving his life. But actually he saved me rather than the reverse. Through saving him, I saved myself. That winter my depression left me. Helping others in need can make one very happy.'

As Dai listened to the story, told in Chinese but expressing an American way of thinking, he could not help wondering why the priest had chosen to tell it to him. Surely he could not be implying that he had come to China thirty years ago because there was so much misery in China. That, like the seven who lay beneath the gravestones, China held an inexhaustible supply of pitiable, needy Chinese, and coming to their aid could make the priests happy. Or was he saying that Dai ought to follow his example, that if he stayed to help the wounded soldiers in the cellar, he too would feel good?

'All I'm telling you is that that old tramp was sent by God.' Father Engelmann saw a frown had appeared between Dai's eyebrows, but he went on nonetheless. 'God used him to give me inspiration. He wanted me to save myself by saving others. God wants people to help each other especially when they are injured or weak. I hope you will trust in God. It is God you should trust, not weapons, when you are powerless to control your fate, as you are now.'

I must be the smallest congregation the priest has ever had for one of his sermons, Dai thought. But nevertheless something in what Father Engelmann had said touched him. Perhaps he would stay for a day or two more.

Eleven

That night there was a ring on the doorbell of the side entrance. Father Engelmann was in the library, wrapped in his goose-down coat. He pulled aside the blackout curtain and saw Fabio hurry to the door and hold a conversation with whoever it was outside.

'Can you tell me what the matter is? . . . This is an American church! . . . We have no food or fuel! . . .' But with every sentence, all Fabio got in reply was another ring on the doorbell, the rings becoming increasingly angry and impatient, frequently interrupting him before he had finished as if engaging him in an argument.

Father Engelmann rushed to the door of the workshop

building and made sure it was firmly locked. Then it occurred to him that it was actually more of a risk to keep the door locked because the intruders would realise there was something inside worth locking up, and might break in, thus putting the girls hidden in the attic in greater danger. He took the bunch of keys which hung from his belt and, with trembling hands, tried one after another until the door finally opened. He fumbled his way through the darkness and called up to the trapdoor in the ceiling: 'Listen, girls! Whatever happens, you are not to make a sound or to come down!'

He knew they had heard him, so he turned and made for the kitchen.

'The Japanese are here,' he called down to the women and soldiers. 'You're not to make a sound. Fabio and I will deal with everything!'

One of the women began to ask something, but then fell silent. Someone must have clamped their hand over her mouth or quietly ordered her to shut up.

Father Engelmann pulled a barrel over the trapdoor to the cellar and prepared himself to meet the newcomers. About five paces from the side door he stopped and took a deep breath. Then he ordered Fabio, who was still shouting futile questions, to open up.

Fabio turned to look at Father Engelmann, and was reassured by the older priest's unruffled bearing and words. It was almost as if the priest had been waiting for this moment, as if he was challenging any spirit or human being not to be quelled and retreat in the face of the divinity which inspired him.

As a result, when the door opened, the Japanese were met by a sage old greybeard who appeared ready to bestow forgiveness to all his flock, of whatever colour and character, guilty and innocent alike. The anger which had accumulated in the Japanese soldiers as they rang the doorbell seemed to evaporate at Father Engelmann's all-embracing smile.

'We're hungry!' said the junior officer who was in command, in comical English.

'So are we,' said Father Engelmann. And he added, with an air of extending compassion to all hungry beings, 'We're out of water too.'

'We want to come in,' said the officer.

'I'm sorry, this is an American church. You should treat it as if it were American territory, sir,' said Father Engelmann, still with a smile on his face.

'We've been into the American embassy.'

Father Engelmann had heard that the Japanese had broken

into the embassy, the safest place in the Safety Zone, shooting and plundering everything they could lay their hands on. The cars belonging to the ambassador and to expatriate Americans had all been taken too. It seemed his old church, far away from the city centre, was indeed safer than the Safety Zone.

'We're coming in to look for food!' the officer yelled at him.

The seven or eight soldiers standing behind him seemed to take this as a signal to charge and pressed through the doorway into the courtyard.

'Now the door's open, we're finished!' whispered Fabio.

'The city walls of Nanking couldn't stop them,' said Father Engelmann. 'Besides, even the women managed to climb over our walls and get in.'

The two clergymen followed on the heels of the Japanese as they entered the church. It was pitch dark and more bitterly cold even than outside. The soldiers hesitated on the threshold. The beam of the officer's torch illuminated the figure of Christ hanging from the cross above the altar then shifted to the unfathomable depths under the roof. Then he drew back, as if afraid of an ambush.

Father Engelmann said in low tones to Fabio, 'As soon as

they start to search the workshop, we must create a diversion and draw them off.'

'What kind of a diversion?'

Father Engelmann pondered. Something less important would have to be sacrificed to protect the most important.

'Go and tell George to start the car.'

Fabio understood instantly. If the Japanese soldiers could loot a car, they would be rewarded by their seniors and could barter the car with Chinese collaborators for food and valuables that were easier than a car to carry away, such as gold, silver and jewellery. They had been in occupation only a few days and already a thriving black market had grown up.

As soon as the soldiers opened the door to the workshop, a car engine was heard reverberating loudly through the courtyard. It purred smoothly and was clearly an engine of quality. The soldiers flashed their torches around the court-yard to see where the car was and spotted the garage. They also spotted the figure of George, lying underneath, appar-ently engaged in some repairs.

One soldier gave George a kick in the head. 'Who's that?' he shouted in English.

George's muffled voice came from beneath the car. 'I'm

fixing it!' His English was even harder to understand than the officer's.

'Come out, George,' Father Engelmann said.

Fabio had told George to stick to English and had rehearsed what he was to say. But when George slowly crawled out from under the old Ford, he had completely forgotten his lines. His oil-streaked face was filled with panic.

'Who are you?' asked the Japanese officer.

'He's the cook and handyman,' said Father Engelmann, placing himself between George and the officer.

The officer turned to Father Engelmann. 'We need to borrow the car.'

'This is not my private property,' the priest answered. 'It's not mine to lend you. It belongs to the mission.' He was well aware that there was no point arguing: the car was lost. But he thought that if he prevaricated, he could persuade the Japanese that the church held nothing else of value. 'So perhaps you could ask your commanding officer for a receipt for the loan which I can pass to the finance department of the church mission.'

The officer looked at him as if to say, *And are you living on the moon? Don't you know anything about war?* But instead he said in English: 'We'll get you a receipt as soon as we get to the occupying forces HQ.'

As Father Engelmann and Fabio continued to protest that the car was not theirs to lend, the soldiers ignored them and pushed the Ford out of its garage. The officer sat in the driver's seat and pumped the throttle a few times, pondered a moment, then started the engine. His men whooped with joy at having landed such valuable booty. Hollering like tribesmen, they ran after it out of the church compound.

Fabio and Father Engelmann breathed audible sighs of relief. George stared after them. He hardly dared believe that the war had really come to the church, brushed past him and left.

'They think they've taken our most valuable possession,' said Father Engelmann. 'We should be safer now.'

Twelve

Shujuan and the other girls had no idea what had been going on. After the priest had shouted, 'You're not to make a sound or to come down,' they had not let out a whisper. They had not even crowded around the windows as they had done on previous days. Where the blackout curtains joined, they could see torches flicking back and forth like small search-lights. But they lay motionless on their beds.

It was only when they heard the Ford start up that some of the bolder girls crept to the window and peered through the gaps in the curtains. They could not see much but they could hear a chorus of shouts. In Japanese.

Then there were cheers.

The Japanese Army had finally arrived, and then had driven away with the Ford which Father Engelmann had had for ten years. These were the only two facts that were clear to them.

The girls sat up, wrapped in their quilts, and debated what would happen next time the Japanese came, who they would shoot and what else they would do. Shujuan remembered what she had overheard when she was standing above the cellar holding the shovel, embers glinting in the hot ash.

'They say that when the Japanese soldiers march into the Safety Zone, what they're looking for are young girls,' she said.

'How do they know? They're in hiding here!' said Sophie.

'The Japanese are on the hunt for any females – old women, little girls of seven or eight, anyone!' Shujuan said.

'You're just spreading rumours!' said Xiaoyu.

'Ask Father Engelmann if you think I'm spreading rumours!' retorted Shujuan. 'He has seen it happen.'

'Just rumours!' shouted Xiaoyu. She had a way of shouting down news that she did not want to hear.

Shujuan said nothing. She knew her friendship with Xiaoyu was over. This was the final break. Nanking was filled with misery, the dead and the living were all miserable, but she was young enough to feel this widespread misery was vague and insubstantial. Losing her best friend, on the other hand, was real misery. Xiaoyu was heartless. All pretty girls were heartless, just like that pretty woman down in the cellar, Yumo.

The other girls went to sleep. Xiaoyu moved herself away from Shujuan and squeezed in next to Anna. Shujuan lay there for a while, then got up and dressed. But just as she was opening the trapdoor, she heard Xiaoyu say: 'What are you doing, Shujuan?'

'Nothing to do with you,' said Shujuan. She had her pride, and she wanted the other girls to understand that what she was really saying was: *If you don't want to be my friend any more, Xiaoyu, then that's fine. I couldn't care less. I don't want you for a friend either. You think you can buy our friendship with that rubbish about your father coming to rescue you? Well, where's he been all this time then? Even if he's as clever at rescuing people as you say, thanks, but I don't care!*

'Don't go down, Shujuan!' a couple of the girls said.

'Just ignore her!' said Xiaoyu angrily.

The other two girls obediently ignored Shujuan.

Shujuan felt as if she had been exiled. But at least that

left her free to do what she wanted. Down in the courtyard, she pottered around until she got to the kitchen door. Maybe she could find something to eat. Maybe the charcoal embers would still have some life in them and she could put them in a warming pan and warm up her frozen feet. They had not had any hot water to wash their feet for days. As she got to the kitchen door, she heard a man and a woman talking in low tones. The man was George, she could tell straight away.

'I can't, really I can't. If I do some for you, Father Engelmann will kick me out.'

'Just cook me a couple of potatoes! He won't know . . .' said the woman.

'I'll have to beg for a living if he kicks me out!'

'I'll keep you.'

It was Hongling, Shujuan could hear.

'Just five . . . !'

'No!'

'Three!'

'Shut up or I'll throttle you!'

'And I'll bite you!'

The voices were replaced by some sort of snuffling noises and Shujuan beat a hasty retreat. These sluts couldn't sell their rotten bodies for money here, so they were selling them for potatoes instead. When she had moved back half a dozen paces, she found herself between two of the ventilation shafts. Down in the cellar, she could hear someone crying. She sat cross-legged and looked down one of them.

It was not just one woman – Nani and two others were weeping, the stupid way people did when they had been drinking. Yumo was drunk too. A bowl of wine in one hand, she was trying to console the three other women. They were clearly wreaking havoc on the church's wine stores.

'I saw those Japanese soldiers!' Nani was wailing. 'They were ferocious! They'd fuck you to death!'

'You can't have seen them, only their feet!' Yumo teased her.

'I did!'

'All right, all right, you saw them . . .'

'I want to get out, I want to go. I don't want to stay in this fucking hole waiting for them to come and fuck me!' Nani was getting maudlin.

Sergeant Major Li's voice came from a corner Shujuan could not see. 'This dressing's fucking useless!'

'Show it to me.' Major Dai's voice sounded weak and weary.

She shifted to the other shaft and, when she looked down it, saw Cardamom kneeling beside the boy soldier, Wang Pusheng. He was bare-chested, with a woman's padded jacket around his shoulders. His face looked different, his features ominously swollen out of all recognition.

'What's he saying?' Sergeant Major Li asked Cardamom.

'He says it hurts.'

'It stinks. The dressing needs to be changed. It'll be painful but he'll just have to put up with it!' said Li.

Cardamom stood up, snatched the bowl from Li and took a sip of wine. Then she knelt down again and squirted the mouthful into the boy's mouth.

'Drink some wine and it won't hurt,' she said. Then, little by little, sipping and squirting the liquid into his mouth, she made him drink the rest of the bowlful. There was silence in the room, as if everyone was suffering along with Wang Pusheng. From Shujuan's vantage point, she could see the boy struggling feebly, either because he did not like the unaccustomed taste of the wine or because he was trying to evade Cardamom's lips. He may have been at death's door, but he could still feel embarrassment.

Caradamom dressed his wound, and then fetched her *pipa*. It only had one string left, the thickest one which gave a deep bass note. Cardamom plucked it and hummed a tune. 'Do you like it?' she asked Wang Pusheng.

'Yes,' he said.

'Really?'

'Uh-huh.'

'I'll play for you every day.'

'Thank you . . .'

'Don't thank me, marry me,' said Cardamom.

This time no one mocked her.

'I'll go home with you and work in the fields,' Cardamom said, as if she were a child playing at happy families.

'We don't have any fields,' said Wang Pusheng with a smile.

'Well, what have you got then?'

'We don't have anything.'

'Then I'll play the *pipa* for you every day. I'll play and you'll walk with a stick and beg for food, and we'll give it to your mum,' said Cardamom, full of happy daydreams.

'I haven't got a mother.'

Cardamom was startled. She put her arms around Wang Pusheng and they saw her shoulders jerking. For the first time, Cardamom was crying a woman's tears.

Nani, no longer maudlin, wept quietly along with several of the other women.

After a while, Cardamom stopped, picked up the *pipa* and flung it away. 'It's useless! It's made everyone cry! With only one string it sounds worse than plucking cotton wool!'

Shujuan noticed a change in the women. They knew now that nowhere was safe, nowhere was off-limits to the occupying troops. They had imagined this was a secret corner that the war had, by some lucky fluke, overlooked. But the arrival of the Japanese soldiers this evening had disabused them of that idea. Three hundred thousand soldiers had seeped into every corner of Nanking, every alleyway, every home, and every nook and cranny.

Shujuan got up to go, and found her eyes were wet with tears too. She had actually let those women make her cry!

It might have been the dying boy soldier, or perhaps it was Cardamom's childish marriage proposal that got to her. Or maybe it was the tune that Cardamom was strumming on the single *pipa* string, a familiar one south of the Yangtze River, called 'Picking Tea'. Now that southern China had fallen, all that was left of it was 'Picking Tea', played on a single string.

Thirteen

When the women in the cellar woke up in the morning, Cardamom's bed was empty. George said that, when he got up at daybreak to heat water, he had seen her staggering drunkenly around the courtyard. He had tried to persuade her to go to bed, but she had ordered him to go to her house to get three new *pipa* strings. She said the *pipa* sounded awful, because it only had one string left. How could he go? George said. He didn't know where she lived. She had replied that everyone knew how to get to the Qin Huai River. The house she belonged to was right on the riverbank, and her *pipa* strings were kept in the drawer of her dresser; he couldn't possibly miss them. George tried to pacify her by saying he would go once it got light, but she said she could not wait. Wang Pusheng would be dead by then. She wanted to be able to play to him properly.

George had gone about his chores thinking she was back down in the cellar sleeping off her drunkenness. He was sure that, when morning came, she would have forgotten her mad idea.

Cardamom's absence affected everyone in the compound. They were all on edge. When, at nightfall, she still hadn't returned, Father Engelmann and Fabio went up to the attic to talk to the girls. The two clegymen had to stoop uncomfortably in the confined space, as if they were praying.

Fabio spoke first. He told the girls there was no news of Cardamom.

Father Engelmann interrupted him. 'It's no good trying to screen you girls. We have to assume the worst. That Cardamom has been taken by the Japanese and subjected to who knows what tortures . . .'

As the girls listened, the blood drained from their faces. Now that violence might have been inflicted on someone they knew, it suddenly became very real. They had hated Cardamom. They had fought with her. Now they thought of her as a young girl with a most unjust fate. She had been sold from brothel to brothel like a little dog. Would she have been willing to do what she did had she had a choice? Possibly not. People always said whores had no heart, and yet Cardamom risked her life to get *pipa* strings just so she could play a better tune for Wang Pusheng. As they sat dull-faced listening to Father Engelmann, they asked in their minds: Why Cardamom? She was too young. Gradually, tears welled up in their eyes. They'd rather God had swapped any of those prostitutes in the cellar for Cardamom.

'I want you to get your things together and move down to the cellar straight away,' said Father Engelmann. 'Fabio and I and some other teachers hid from the fighting down there during the 1927 Nanking Incident. We were safe even though both armies ransacked the church compound several times. The cellar is much safer than the attic.'

'Is that really appropriate?' asked Fabio doubtfully. 'Those women are completely intemperate in everything they say and do —'

'There's nothing more important than safety,' said Father Engelmann firmly. 'Off you go, children.'

By dinner time, the girls had moved to their new home and the soldiers were ensconced in the workshop. If they were discovered by the Japanese, the priest would just have to do his best to explain that they were wounded civilians. Whether or not he would be believed was in God's hands. It was Dai who suggested the move; it was clear that he felt the men had no choice in the matter. They must protect the women and girls.

* * *

A curtain still divided the cellar in two, but the side that had belonged to the soldiers was now where the schoolgirls arranged their bedding. That night they ate their meagre supper in the cellar rather than the refectory.

Their meal was interrupted by Fabio calling down from the kitchen.

'Xu Xiaoyu, come upstairs please.'

The girls looked at each other. Had the impossible happened? Had Xiaoyu's father actually managed to come and rescue her?

They crowded round one of the ventilation shafts and, peering upwards, saw Xiaoyu's pretty feet come to a halt before a gleaming pair of men's leather shoes. Then they heard a choked cry: 'Dad!'

Shujuan learned later that in order to rescue his daughter,

Xiaoyu's father had sold one of his stores in Macau. Then he had returned to Nanking, but discovered that money was worth nothing; the Japanese did not need money to get what they wanted. He was a good businessman so he went into business with the Japanese, putting antiques, jewellery and paintings their way, selling his integrity and his conscience. Finally he got the laissez-passer he needed and could get his daughter out. Getting into Nanking was as hard as getting to heaven, but leaving it was as difficult as getting to the universe beyond.

Xiaoyu crouched down and called through the shaft to the watching faces below: 'My dad's come to get me!' She sounded as if she were saying: 'An angel's come to get me!'

No one said anything. Even Anna, whom Xiaoyu had promised to take with her, was glum-faced and silent. It was wishful thinking to imagine that someone this lucky would remember her promises.

Xiaoyu got to her feet and the girls heard her say: 'I want to take two classmates with me, Dad!'

'Don't be ridiculous!' said her father roughly.

'I do!'

Her father hesitated. The girls held their breath. Finally he said: 'All right. Who do you want to take?'

Xiaoyu went through the kitchen and climbed down the ladder. Fifteen girls stood there, not daring to make a sound. Xiaoyu had the power of life and death over them. The women on the other side of the curtain were just as silent, as if the choice of who were going to be the lucky ones mattered enormously to them too.

Xiaoyu looked first at one, then at another. Most of them knew they had no prospect of being chosen, even though they would gladly have jumped at the chance of being a servant in the Xu family household.

'Anna,' said Xiaoyu.

Anna, flushed with the honour of being chosen, slowly stood up and went to stand beside her friend.

Xiaoyu looked at the remaining faces, which were increasingly anxious and despondent. Shujuan was full of regret that she had not made it up with Xiaoyu, but it was too late now. She could only feign indifference as to whether she lived or died.

'Xiaoyu, you said you'd take me with you!' Sophie whined.

Shujuan was aghast at Sophie's self-abasement. She turned to look at her – and met Xiaoyu's eyes instead. Xiaoyu's gaze was kindly, she discovered, but in a superior way. Shujuan just had to open her mouth and call her name, it seemed to say, and Xiaoyu would be content to forget all about the past. Shujuan could be best friends again with her old companion, Xiaoyu, the girl who had always got the same marks as her through all their school years.

Shujuan felt frantic. She could not open her mouth to speak, though her eyes were still fixed on Xiaoyu. Only she knew how degraded, how hopeless, she felt at that moment.

But then Xiaoyu turned her gaze away. She had toyed with Shujuan's feelings again. And she was still toying with her classmates.

'Let's draw lots,' said Xiaoyu.

She pulled a page from her notebook and tore it into fourteen pieces. On one of these pieces, she drew a flower.

'I don't want to. Draw lots among the rest of you,' said Shujuan, turning her back valiantly.

'Come on,' said Xiaoyu. 'My dad can't take all of you . . .' She seemed almost to be begging Shujuan.

Shujuan shook her head.

The winner was one of the girls who had hardly even exchanged a word with Xiaoyu, and she was duly taken away by Xiaoyu's father. The remaining thirteen girls were left sharing a bar of chocolate which he had brought with him. To be precise, twelve of them shared it. Shujuan volunteered to give up her portion to the rest. If Xiaoyu thought she could buy off the ones she had abandoned with sweets, she had another think coming. Shujuan would not give her the satisfaction.

On the other side of the curtain, Nani was heard muttering: 'That girl's dad must have money . . . he must be very, very rich. If you have money, you can make anything happen.'

'Didn't your Wu have a bit of money? The one who butchered ducks for a living?'

'Nani let him get away. She didn't squeeze him tight enough with her legs!' said Hongling.

'Keep your filthy mouths shut!' said Yumo.

'Last year, he said he wanted to pay back the bond on me and make me his second wife,' said Nani.

'You're a complete idiot! You fancied yourself as a duchess but you ended up as a duck!'

'Even people's ducks have been killed by the Japs! If a Jap saw a stupid duck like Nani, wouldn't he like a bit of her?'

'Just let him try it on, I'd give him one in the balls!' Nani said angrily.

'Will you keep your mouth shut, Nani?!' Yumo intervened once more.

A few moments later, Nani began to cry. 'I'm not that stupid! Being with Wu was better than being in this hellhole! The way we're stuck down here now, we might all end up like Cardamom!'

On the other side of the curtain, the girls huddled close to each other.

Suddenly Nani's crying stopped. It sounded like someone had put a quilt over her head.

The girls squeezed up together and slept. Later that night, they did not know what time it was, there was a commotion from the women on the other side of the curtain. The doorbell was ringing.

Fourteen

As soon as Father Engelmann heard the doorbell he went to the kitchen and whispered down to the women and girls through the ventilation shaft. 'Don't worry. Fabio and I will deal with them. Don't let me hear a single sound out of any of you.'

Then he went to the workshop and gently pushed open the door. He was startled to find Major Dai standing inside, looking grimly ready to fight to the death. Behind him, the tables had been pushed together to make a bed for Wang Pusheng, who was drifting feverishly in and out of consciousness.

'You're not to come out unless it's absolutely necessary.

Fabio and I will get rid of them,' said the priest, patting Dai on the shoulder and smiling slightly.

Then he went to the side entrance, where the bell was ringing . . . and ringing . . . and ringing. It was foolish to open up to night visitors, but even more foolish to refuse. Father Engelmann's thoughts were in a whirl. Finally Fabio emerged, his breath sour from the rice wine he had drunk.

Father Engelmann opened the small spyhole in the door, and moved his head to the left, out of range of any bayonet which might be thrust through from the outside. A bayonet did indeed come through so it was lucky his eyes were not in the way. The headlights of the vehicle outside streamed under the door.

'Would you mind telling me what it is you want?' asked Father Engelmann with the utmost courtesy, in English.

'Open up!' came a voice in Chinese. It was said that Japanese soldiers and junior officers had all learned a few words of Chinese during their week of occupation: 'Open up!' 'Get out!' 'Food!' 'Petrol!' 'Sing-song girls!'

'And how may I help you?' Father Engelmann's monotone Chinese was designed to pacify the most aggressive of intruders.

He was answered by the butts of their guns. They pounded on the door so hard that a crack opened up between the two panels. Light from the car headlamps outside streamed through the gap.

'This is an American church and we bought this land decades ago. Letting you in is like letting you onto American soil,' Fabio expostulated in his thick Yangzhou accent. If the Japanese were not swayed by Engelmann's genteel English, perhaps they would take notice of something a bit tougher.

A Chinese voice answered.

'The Imperial Japanese Army has accurate reports that you are harbouring Chinese soldiers –'

'Nonsense!' Fabio cut the man short. 'The Japanese troops have been using that excuse to loot all across Nanking. Do you think we're still taken in by nonsense like that?'

There was a moment's silence outside the door as the collaborator-interpreter translated.

'Father,' he began again, 'these people have guns. Please don't try their patience!'

Father Engelmann heard a movement behind him and looked round to see shadowy figures toting guns emerging from behind the church. The Japanese must have discovered they could save their breath by just getting in over the wall.

'They're already in,' said Father Engelmann in low tones. 'We need to be ready for the worst.'

Fabio blocked the entrance. 'You're trespassing!' he shouted. 'We've already told you, there are no Chinese soldiers here! I'm going to the Safety Zone now, to fetch Mr Rabe –'

There was a gunshot and Fabio cried out. He felt as if he had been knocked sideways by a punch to the left shoulder. As he dropped to the icy flagstones, he felt something hot spurt from the wound. He heard a furious shout from Father Engelmann: 'How dare you shoot an American priest!' and Engelmann rushed over to him. 'Fabio!'

'I'm all right, Father,' said Fabio. Looking at the elderly priest, he suddenly recalled the man who, twenty years ago, had descended from the lecture podium and made straight for him. Twenty years ago, Father Engelmann had seen in him an apostle whom he would take under his wing. Yet, twenty years later, Father Engelmann, in his impersonal, distant, even eccentric way, actually depended on Fabio rather than the reverse.

Just then, a couple of dozen Japanese soldiers burst through the entrance doors and rushed towards the church.

Father Engelmann hurried after them. 'There are absolutely no Chinese soldiers here. Please get out.'

Fabio strode off to the far end of the compound without bothering to examine his wound.

In the printing workshop, Li and Dai had prepared themselves for a fight. Li stood behind the door, holding a mallet which he had found in the workshop toolbox. He would first let them come in, then club them from behind and seize a gun. Then he and Major Dai would engage them in pitched battle using any arms they were able to seize from the Japanese.

Major Dai was squatting behind a table turned on its side to face the door. He was holding a pick used to break up lumps of coal. If he and Li let two soldiers in and then shut the door on them, they could attack, the advantage (their only one) being that they would take the Japanese unawares.

Then Dai realised the import of the priests' denial that there were Chinese soldiers in the compound.

Taking his shoes off, he said in low tones to Li: 'Put the mallet down.'

'Aren't we going to put up a fight?'

'We can't fight. Just think about it. The moment we do, we're proving that the Father has been sheltering soldiers.'

'So what?'

'So the Japs will search all the church buildings from

cellar to attic, and they might even burn them to the ground. What will happen to the girls and women then?'

'So what do we do?'

'Take off our clothes and go to sleep. Pretend we're civilians.'

Sergeant Major Li threw down the mallet and was just groping his way to the makeshift bed when the door was flung open and torch beams flashed around the room.

He almost picked up the mallet again.

'They're members of our congregation. Their house was burned down and they had nowhere to go so they sought refuge with us,' said Father Engelmann imperturbably.

'Out!'

The Japanese officer's yell was translated by the interpreter in a perfect mimicry of his tone of voice.

Dai slowly got to his feet, with the grumpy air of someone whose sleep has been disturbed.

'Hurry up!'

Dai put on Fabio's old coat which, like the pullover he had on underneath, was obviously not his. It hung far too long and loose on him.

Sergeant Major Li was wearing an old padded coat belonging to George, which was too short, reaching only to his knees. He had one of Fabio's hats on too. It came down over his eyebrows.

'Who's that?'

The torch beam settled on Wang Pusheng, lying on his makeshift bed.

'My nephew,' said Sergeant Major Li. 'He's seriously ill. He's had a high fever for days –'

Before he had finished speaking, two soldiers dragged the boy from under his quilt. Wang Pusheng sagged insensibly between them. But his breath came hoarse and rapid, as if the rough treatment they were giving him had restored some life to his frail young body.

'He's only a child, and he's seriously ill!' Father Engelmann protested.

The soldiers paid no attention, and dragged Wang Pusheng out into the courtyard. The priest followed behind, hoping to plead the boy's cause, when the swish of a bayonet stopped him in his tracks. Slashes appeared in his padded coat, releasing a cloud of white goose down which danced in the torchlight. Just a little deeper and the bayonet could have pierced his heart. The slash seemed intended as a warning: the bayonet was sharp enough, wasn't it? A thrust to the heart would be just as easy.

The heart was defenceless against a sharp blade like this; there was nowhere for it to hide. The bayonet challenged him, teasing his priest's dignity. Why else should it make such a skittish gesture? However, the priest was not deterred. He continued to follow them, shouting, 'Put him down!'

His violent movements released more goose down from his coat, and a veritable snowstorm formed in his wake.

'For God's sake, put him down!'

He managed to get in front of them, and they finally put Wang Pusheng on the ground, where he lay gasping desperately for breath. Father Engelmann pulled off his coat and laid it over the boy.

The Japanese officer prodded the boy with the toe of his boot and said something. The interpreter said in Chinese: 'He's got a bayonet wound.'

'That's right,' said Father Engelmann.

'Where did that happen?'

'In his home.'

'No, it happened on the execution ground. He's an escaped POW. He was rescued and brought here.'

'What execution ground?' asked the priest.

'The place where we've been executing Chinese POWs,' said the officer, and the interpreter rendered his barely suppressed indignation as well as the words.

'What? You've been executing Chinese POWs?' exclaimed Father Engelmann. 'Forgive my ignorance. I didn't know that the Japanese Army had exempted itself from the Geneva Convention.'

The officer was momentarily silenced by Father Engelmann's words. Then he spoke to the interpreter.

'The officer says it's obvious you've been sheltering Chinese soldiers. You can't deny it, can you?'

'How can they possibly be soldiers?' exclaimed the priest, gesturing to Dai and Li.

At that moment, one of the Japanese pushed a middle-aged Chinese man forward. The interpreter said, 'This is one of the burial team hired by the Japanese Army. He says that two POWs who weren't killed were brought here.' He turned to the man. 'Do you recognise them?'

'Of course I do!' said the man enthusiastically. 'He's one,' and he pointed at Dai.

Fabio swore violently at him. 'You scum of the earth!'

Two of the soldiers fell on Dai and seized him by the arm. Dai submitted as they twisted his arms behind his back, although this caused an excruciating stab of pain to the wound in his left side.

Father Engelmann confronted the gravedigger. 'You're lying! This is the first time you've set eyes on this man.'

'Are you sure you recognise him?' asked the Japanese officer through the interpreter.

'Does he hell!' shouted Fabio. 'He's just trying to save his own skin.'

The officer ordered the two soldiers to escort Dai away. Father Engelmann tried again to intervene but the officer slapped him across the face and the priest staggered.

'You've got the wrong man!' Sergeant Major Li suddenly spoke. He was leaning on his makeshift crutch, dragging his wounded leg, but struggled to draw himself up to his full height. He turned to the gravedigger. 'Look at me! Aren't I the one you rescued?'

'I never rescued anyone!' shouted the gravedigger, panic-stricken.

'Didn't you say you recognised two people? Then what about me?' said Li, cocking his thumb at himself in a ruffian-like fashion.

'They're both ordinary civilians!'

Engelmann knew this was his last chance to save them.

Come what may, he would protect Dai. His conversations with this young soldier had drawn the pair of them close. He wanted to carry on talking to him . . . Then the Japanese officer balled his hand into a fist, gave an almighty swing, and Engelmann felt another stinging blow on the face.

At this point, George emerged from behind the kitchen as if he were going to wipe the blood from the priest's nose and mouth. When the Japanese had forced their way in, George had crept towards the courtyard and ducked down behind a pile of firewood to watch. George did not believe in heroics. He would prefer a rascally life to a good death. Especially now that he and Hongling were getting on so well, a rascally life seemed to offer countless pleasures. But as he saw Father Engelmann's coat slashed, and the priest beaten about the face, he instinctively grabbed a stick of firewood. How could these Jap scum treat the Reverend Father like this? They were not good enough to empty the Father's chamber pot! Then he put the stick down again; there was no point tangling with twenty Japs armed with loaded rifles. He stayed crouching where he was, bolstered in his belief that it was best not risk his life, although also berating himself for disloyalty. Father Engelmann had looked after him since he was a boy of thirteen, feeding and clothing him and teaching him to read and write. He had persisted with his education even after it became clear that he was not convert material. True, the Father was rather a dull man (though that was not his fault), and did not seem fond of him, rather the reverse. In fact, the Father was more affectionate to the pony that had turned the water wheel at their well. Still, without Father Engelmann, George would have gone from being a child beggar to a grown-up beggar until finally, if luck was on his side, he died an old beggar. Without the dry-as-dust old priest, George would never have become a church cook. He could never have swaggered round with the key to the food store hanging from his waistband, and had the delectable Hongling running after him. He was thinking these thoughts when he saw the officer slap Engelmann round the head for the second time, so hard that the priest must have lost some teeth. His own teeth ached in sympathy.

As he ran to help the priest, he was collared by one of the soldiers.

'He's the church cook!' said Fabio.

'Do you recognise this man?' the Japanese officer asked the gravedigger.

The gravedigger scrutinised George's face, pallid in the torch beam. He looked as if he was going to identify him, but then gave an evasive grunt by way of an answer.

Father Engelmann spat the blood from his mouth through loosened teeth. 'He's an orphan. I adopted the boy seven years ago.'

The officer asked the gravedigger again: 'Who else is a Chinese soldier here?'

The gravedigger took a torch from one of the soldiers and scanned the faces of all the Chinese men.

'I've already told you, any men I've taken in are ordinary civilians, and members of our congregation,' said Father Engelmann.

The gravedigger shone his torch into Li's face. 'I recognise him. He's one,' he said.

'You fool!' shouted Fabio at the gravedigger. 'You've just made it all up! You're even saying our cook's a soldier!'

George, grown a little paunchy from the perks of his kitchen job, stood stock-still, not daring even to blink. Only his eyes flickered shiftily back and forth.

The Japanese officer took off one white glove and traced a circle on George's forehead with his forefinger. He was feeling for the slight indentation made by an army cap, but George thought he was marking the best place to shoot him and instinctively ducked out of the way. Infuriated, the officer drew his sword with a swish. George covered his head with his hands and made a run for it. There was a shot, and he fell to the ground.

'Leave him alone, he's innocent!' shouted Major Dai. 'I'm a Chinese soldier. Take me away!'

Fabio tried to help George up. The cook was jerking spasmodically, although increasingly feebly. The bullet had hit him in the back and come out of his chest, piercing his windpipe. With each breath, the air wheezed through the bullet hole and his plump body gradually deflated.

George's thrashings brought him up against one of the ventilation shafts. Shujuan pressed the back of her hand to her mouth, to stop herself crying out as Sophie had. One of the other, more courageous girls held Sophie tightly in her arms and gently stroked her as if she were her mother.

The Japanese officer looked intently at Dai. A professional soldier could always smell another professional. He felt this Chinese man did indeed seem to have the blood-thirsty air of a good soldier.

He turned to Father Engelmann and said complacently through the interpreter: 'So, Father, don't talk to me about

American neutrality here. Do you still maintain that you are not sheltering enemies of our army?'

'I didn't ask his permission when I broke in. Leave the Father out of it,' said Dai.

'He's not an enemy of the Japanese Army,' said Father Engelmann. 'He's completely unarmed now, so of course he counts as an innocent civilian.'

But the officer signalled abruptly with one white-gloved hand, ordering his men to take the three surviving Chinese men away.

'You said you were only taking two away!' shouted Fabio. 'You've already killed one of our employees!'

'If we discover we've got the wrong men, we'll return them to you,' replied the officer.

'And if you kill them in error?' said Fabio.

'In a war, there are always many people killed in error.'

Father Engelmann stood in front of the Japanese officer. 'I'm warning you one more time, this is American territory. You've killed a man here and are taking innocent men into detention. Have you thought of the consequences?'

'And do you know how our superiors evade those "consequences"? They maintain they are only the uncontrolled actions of individuals within the armed forces, and those individuals will be subjected to military discipline, although in fact no individual is ever investigated. Do you understand, Father? Individuals lose control all the time in wartime.' The officer spoke easily and, just as easily, the interpreter rendered his words into Chinese.

Father Engelmann was silent. He knew the officer was telling the truth.

Major Dai spoke up. 'I must apologise, Father, for trespassing and causing you unnecessary trouble.' He raised his right arm in a salute.

A Japanese soldier started kicking Wang Pusheng and shouting, 'Get up! Get up!'

The boy moaned in agony.

'I've never seen soldiers behave as brutally as you!' Father Engelmann protested, attempting to pull off the soldier whose foot was poised to kick Wang Pusheng in the belly. 'For God's sake, spare this child's life!'

The officer brandished his sword to keep Father Engelmann at arm's length. At this, Sergeant Major Li, who was standing close by, was suddenly galvanised into action. He hurled himself on the officer, his left arm hooked around the other's neck, his right hand reaching for the officer's windpipe. For a moment, no one moved. The Japanese soldiers dared not fire in case they hit their commanding officer. Then they launched themselves at Li with their bayonets. Again and again, the officer's subordinates twisted their bayonets in Li's guts, but with each terrible stab, his grip on the officer's neck tightened. The officer was crumpling, almost unconscious, but this climactic effort was Li's last – then it was over.

His hands stiffened, and his eyes glazed over. Only his teeth were still bared, the strong, uneven teeth of a Chinese peasant used to coarse, humble fare. The sort of teeth which, clenched on a curse, were enough to make the officer quail.

The officer gave a hoarse command and his soldiers began a search. The compound was filled with criss-crossing torch beams. Father Engelmann remained where he stood uttering a passionate, silent prayer. Fabio watched panic-stricken as the beams searched the printing workshop. Upstairs, sixteen beds all stood in place, and they, as well as sixteen choir robes, would all offer clues to the Japanese. If they made the connection between these black gowns and the young bodies which they clothed, the consequences would be unimaginable.

It was not hard for the searchers to spot the trapdoor

to the attic, and Fabio soon saw the torch beams filter through the gaps between the blackout curtains.

The soldiers who went to search the kitchen and refectory had returned empty-handed. Fabio sighed in relief. He had placed a brazier over the cellar entrance and jammed all their cooking implements into the kitchen so there was scarcely room to move.

In fact, the soldiers had been distracted by something else: they had broken open George's locked store cupboard and pulled out a bag of potatoes and half a bag of flour. Hundreds of thousands of the invading forces had endured hunger and thirst along with the Chinese, so there were cheers when they found the food.

*   *   *

Down below, eyes of all shapes and sizes stared unblinking at the ceiling, and watched the torchlight which filtered down through the edges of the trapdoor.

Several of the girls were moaning in terror. Yumo hissed in her fiercest voice: 'If you young misses make another sound, I'll come over and kill you!'

Nani smeared her face with coal dust. Jade looked at her,

then groped around until her hands too were covered in cobwebby dust, which she smeared all over her face. Yumo smiled wryly to herself. Had they not heard that the Japs were making 'comfort women' out of seventy-year-old grannies? Only Hongling ignored the light coming through the trapdoor. She sat staring into the darkness, giving occasional sobs. She could hardly believe that George had just been transformed from a living being to a bloody lump of flesh. She had been with countless men, but only this one, with whom she had snatched a few moments of pleasure amid the horrors of war, had aroused such tenderness in her. And now George, with his protruding ears and his wordless smiles, was gone. It was too much for her to take in. George used to say: 'Better a rascally life than a good death.' But now not even this cheerful, obdurate and single-minded 'rascal' was to be granted his desire. My poor George, Hongling thought numbly.

Yumo's heart was pounding for Major Dai. The night before, she had climbed the church's ruined bell tower with him. They had scrambled up the bomb-damaged steps with Dai stretching out his hand to steady her in the darkness, saying, 'Let's explore as if they were ancient ruins.'

The wind up in the tower was different, colder, but

somehow freer. The destruction had created a jagged space into which humans had to mould themselves. Dai brought out a pair of pocket binoculars. He looked around, then passed them to her. In the moonlight, she could see the dark streets; alleyways branched off them, sprouting with dwellings like leaves. All these houses looked as if they were burned out. It was only the intermittent gunfire that told them this was not some desolate, long-abandoned city devoid of human habitation, and that there were armed prowlers on the hunt out there.

'Your home must be in that direction,' said Major Dai, thinking she was using the binoculars to find the Qin Huai River and the brothel.

'I wasn't looking for that,' she said with a desolate smile. 'It's not my home.'

After a few moments, he asked what she was thinking about. She was actually thinking that she should ask him where his home was, if he had children and how old his wife was. But these were the kind of questions people asked when they planned to spend a lot of time together.

So she said, 'I was thinking . . . I'd like a cigarette.'

Dai smiled. 'Just what I was thinking,' he said.

They exchanged complicit glances then turned to look out

at the streets and alleyways of the ruined city. If they could hear the cries of the cigarette hawkers down there, it would prove that the city was coming back to life and they could leave, Yumo thought. The cigarette hawkers were a prelude, and would soon be followed by the shouts of the noodle sellers. They could find somewhere nice for an evening meal, and then go and dance the night away in a dance hall.

No doubt Dai was thinking along the same lines because he heaved a sigh and said, 'It must be fate that brought us together. Otherwise, a junior regimental officer like me could never have aspired to a date with you, Miss Yumo.'

'You haven't asked me for a date, so how do you know?'

'Didn't I invite you to come and enjoy the view from up here?' He smiled, and nodded to the destruction around them and the dismal scene beyond.

'Does this count as a date?'

'Of course it does!'

He stood awkwardly, no doubt because his wound hurt him, and shifted so that he stood in front of her. She looked at him in the pale moonlight. She knew just how fatally attractive she was when she looked like that.

'Of course it doesn't,' she said.

'All right, it doesn't count then,' he said. 'We'll wait till the war's over, then I'll take you out to dinner and we'll go dancing.'

'I'll remember that,' she said slowly. 'If you don't keep your word and come and make a date with me, then I'll . . .' Her voice trailed away.

'What'll you do?'

'I'll come and ask you out.'

He laughed. 'A woman asking a man out?'

'It would be the first time in my life I'd asked a man on a date, so you'd better watch out.'

She reached over and gently brushed his cheek with her fingers. It was the touch of a whore. She did not want him to marry her. He must be fed up with women like that. What she wanted him to remember was that she owed him a good time, the kind of top-quality good time that only a whore could give him. And, for her to keep her word and for him to enjoy this sensual feast, he would have to go on living and not engage in senseless, bloody fighting.

'I'll remember.'

'What will you remember? Tell me.'

'I'll remember that the famous beauty of Nanking, Zhao Yumo, is going to invite me out and for that reason I can't die.'

'That's right,' said Yumo with a flirtatious smile. 'But

me, Major Dai. You were planning to leave us, weren't you? I saw it in your eyes. You were going to abandon us to our fate.'

'I was,' said Dai with a wry smile. 'But then I realised something was keeping me here.'

Yumo remembered that wry smile now.

'Stop crying, Hongling,' she whispered sharply. 'You might be heard.'

Hongling saw that Yumo was clutching something. It was a small pair of sewing scissors, no bigger than the palm of her hand but very sharp. She had seen Yumo use them to snip the ends of threads or make paper-cut window decorations. When Hongling was younger, Yumo had used them to trim Hongling's eyelashes. If you did that a few times, it made them grow back thick and up-sweeping, she said. Yumo always kept them with her, together with her few pieces of jewellery.

Yumo had never told any of the other women the story of her scissors. They were her most prized possession. She loved them more now than the diamond ring which her faithless lover had given her. She had had the scissors since she was thirteen years old. The brothel madam had lost her needlework scissors and had beaten her for stealing them.

Then when she found them again, she had given them to Yumo by way of an apology. That was the moment when Yumo had made up her mind that she was going to haul herself up to the top of her profession so she could no longer be humiliated over a pair of scissors.

Above them, the soldiers were still turning the kitchen upside down and muttering unintelligibly among themselves. At every noise from above, a sob would be heard from one of the schoolgirls.

'Give me one half of your scissors, Yumo,' said Nani in a low voice.

Yumo took no notice. No doubt they could be pulled apart but who had the energy for that now? Besides, it would make a noise, it would be asking for trouble. Everyone envied Yumo her scissors. They might only give a nip like that of a dying rabbit, but they were better than nothing.

'No need for scissors, just knee them,' said Jade. 'With a bit of luck and if you're fierce enough, you can do a lot of damage to their privates so long as your knees are not tied.'

Yumo shushed them but Jade continued to whisper advice. Her pimp was a hired thug and he had taught her a few kicks and punches. It was best if your hands were free, she said then you could grab their balls and give a twist, the *y* you got a kernel out of a walnut. A good sharp twist and they would not be fathering any more little Jap animals. Yumo thumped her hard, because the kitchen above had gone quiet.

They stood, or crouched, or sat, completely motionless, their slender fists filled with a fierce energy. Twist as if you're getting the kernel out of a walnut, that's what Jade said, as hard as you can, concentrate all your strength into your palm and fingers, crack, crack . . .

Yumo found the scissors she was holding were slippery with sweat. There was a sob from one of the schoolgirls and Yumo pulled the dividing curtain back, hissing: 'What are you crying about? You've got us for scapegoats, haven't you?' Then she went back to the other side of the curtain and peered up the ventilation shaft. She could see the Japanese soldiers dragging Wang Pusheng's bandage-swathed body towards the entrance.

The boy moaned in pain. 'He won't last more than a couple of days, why are you bothering to —' shouted Dai.

Dai's words were cut short by a loud chopping sound. The night before, Yumo had enticed him to live with a promise of sensual pleasure, and he said he would remember that. ow the head which held that memory dropped to the ground.

There was a sudden croak from the dying boy. 'Fuck you and all your ancestors!'

The interpreter did not translate this country boy's curse.

Wang Pusheng carried on. 'Fuck all your Jap sisters too!'

The interpreter was forced to supply a translation. The Japanese officer then used the sword soaked in Dai's blood to administer a final, gratuitous stab into the festering wound in the boy's abdomen.

Yumo pressed her hands over her ears. The boy's last cry was too distressing.

The torches were switched off and there was a clatter of army boots in the direction of the side door. The truck engine started into life, its roar a final blustering farewell. As it faded into the distance, the women and girls saw the feet of Father Engelmann and Fabio move effortfully, in trepidation. They were shifting the dead bodies.

Yumo burst into tears. She stepped back from the ventilation shaft, one hand still gripping her scissors, the other wiping the tears from her face, smearing it with dust in the process. She had loved Major Dai. And not only him; she was promiscuous in her love, and had given her heart to each of the three soldiers.

Fifteen

At six o'clock the next morning, Father Engelmann led the thirteen girls in a farewell to the three dead soldiers and the cook, George Chen. The girls sang the requiem Mass in low voices. Shujuan was standing at the front. After the Japanese had left, they had occupied themselves in making dozens of white camellias in fine white paper. Now each of the four corpses had a simple wreath of flowers. The girls had carried the wreaths into the nave where the women waited. The women, led by Yumo, had spent the intervening hours washing and dressing the bodies, and shaving their faces. They had put Major Dai's head back with his body and Yumo had wrapped a fine woollen scarf of her own around his neck at the join. As the girls walked in, they were greeted by searching looks from the women.

Shujuan noticed that the prostitutes were all plainly dressed and their pale faces showed no traces of make-up. They had decorated their chignons with white flowers which they had made by tearing up a fragment of cloth. Yumo wore a black velvet cheongsam as if she were a widow. In fact, she wore full mourning garb. As Yumo's eyes met Shujuan's, Shujuan looked away. She didn't feel that hot hatred towards Yumo any more. The whore wasn't worth her hatred. Instead what she felt deep down inside her was an echoing wonder. If creatures like Yumo could go on living, then why not noble men such as Major Dai and Sergeant Major Li?

Father Engelmann wore his grandest cassock and surplice, full of moth holes since he rarely brought it out. He had combed his silver hair back and wore a priest's hat on his head. Holding a heavy crook, he walked to the pulpit.

At seven o'clock, they buried the bodies in the church-yard. It was a cold but clear day. The cemetery had the sharp, fresh smell of cypress. Fabio had worked since before dawn to dig four graves. There was nothing to put between the bodies and the earth but silk lent by the women – scarves, dresses, wraps.

Shujuan stood on the edge of Dai's grave. As the earth started falling on his body wrapped in ridiculously colourful clothing, tears rolled down her face. It seemed so unjust for a hero to receive a funeral like this. After the burial, she let everyone else leave and watched Father Engelmann as he stood by the graves with his head bowed.

Eventually he looked up and noticed her.

'It's so unfair,' she said.

The priest looked her in the eye. 'My child?'

'That I should see all this. So unfair.'

'It is.'

'My parents have been spared all of it.'

'They have. Do you want to say something to me, child?'

Shujuan felt the urge to tell him everything: her misery at the changes in her body, her fury at her parents, her hatred of the Qin Huai women, how she had nearly poured hot ash over them. But there was something in Father Engelmann's knowing eyes that stopped her – as if they were telling to her to reconsider her unhappiness.

*   *   *

Later, Father Engelmann put on shoes with rubber soles more suitable for walking and went to the Safety Zone to report on what had happened. He would enquire, while he was there, whether there was any transport which could smuggle the girls out of Nanking. In the meantime, perhaps they could be taken to John Rabe's house, or could be squeezed in at Dr Robinson's. After what had happened, Father Engelmann felt that the church was now unsafe. He even wondered in trepidation whether the soldiers had smelled the girls. He seemed to remember a girl screaming last night. If only it had been his overwrought nerves which dreamed up that scream.

When Fabio went into the churchyard to tidy the graves, he found Yumo standing beside the mound where Major Dai was buried.

Fabio adjusted the bandage on his arm and turned to look at her. 'Let's go in. It looks like it might snow.'

Yumo flicked the back of her hand over her face. She did not want Fabio to see that she was wiping away tears.

Fabio did not move. He sensed Yumo wanted to stay and said to her: 'Go on in, quick, it's not safe outside.'

She turned towards him. The weeping had turned her big eyes and her nose into small reddened blotches in her wan face. She was no longer beautiful, in fact she was ugly. But, looking at her, Fabio found himself immensely moved. This twenty-five-year-old woman could so easily have been a teacher, a secretary, an ordinary wife. He imagined another scenario, one in which as a young man returned from America, he came across a girl of about ten years old whose master was about to sell her and spent all his savings on buying her. Her name, she would tell him, was Yumo. But it was too late for something like that to happen now – to either of them.

'Do you have any family left?' he asked her now.

'Probably,' she said distractedly. 'Why do you ask?'

'If by any chance something should happen . . . I'm sure it won't, but if it did . . . and you lost touch with them, then I could contact them for you.'

'You mean if by any chance I die?' She smiled bitterly. 'As far as my family go, it makes no difference whether I'm alive or dead.'

Fabio said nothing. His shoulder wound was throbbing painfully.

'All they care about is their opium. Me and my sisters were all sold to buy opium for them.'

'How many sisters do you have?'

'I'm the eldest. I have two younger sisters and a little brother. Before my mother became an addict, I was just like those schoolgirls. I went to a good school. I was at a missionary school for a year.'

She told him briefly how she had been pawned to a distant relative as a child, and how that relative's wife had finally sold her on to the Nanking brothel. She spoke in a flat, dull monotone as if what she was saying was quite ordinary. She told him about the humiliation of being unjustly accused of stealing the scissors, and how the incident had made her determined to get to the top, even of this degrading profession.

She and Fabio had moved into the nave of the church. The smell of incense and candlewax from the requiem Mass still hung in the air.

Yumo sat in the front pew. She casually picked up one of the Bibles placed there for the congregation, then smiled wryly at herself for doing so.

Fabio stood in front of her, one side braced stiffly against the pain from his wound. He was a little discomfited: he was not her father confessor, and she was not one of his flock. As a man used to being self-sufficient, knowing too much about other people felt like a burden and made him uncomfortable.

Suddenly she changed the subject and turned to him. 'And what about you, Father?'

She had confided in him; now she wanted him to do the same.

Somehow, Fabio found himself telling her about how he had stayed in China when his parents died and how he had been brought up by Chinese adoptive parents. It struck him that no one had ever wanted to listen to his story before. As she sat there, he was overcome with the desire to tell her absolutely everything. He went back to the beginning and filled in, in vivid detail, everything he had skated over. She listened in rapt attention. When he told her how anxious and apprehensive he had felt when he first met his American relatives, she smiled compassionately. This really was a woman of great empathy and understanding.

It occurred to Fabio that he might stop drinking if he had someone to tell his troubles to. A listening face like hers was intoxicating enough.

'I never thought I'd ever end up talking to a priest,' said Yumo.

And Fabio had never imagined that he would confide the story of his life to a prostitute.

'Will you stay on here at the church?'

Fabio looked blank. He had always assumed that he would pass the rest of his days here and, when the end came, be buried next to Father Engelmann in the churchyard. But now that Yumo had put the question, he suddenly began to have doubts. They were nebulous, ill-defined doubts but they coexisted with his former certainty. God's existence was nebulous too; especially last night, when the Creator had seemed so completely powerless, as easily cowed as human beings. He looked at the woman who had inspired these doubts in him. He heard himself telling her the story of how he met Father Engelmann. Meanwhile, another part of his mind was elaborating on his daydream: how, at eleven or twelve, the child Yumo might have met a Western youth who spoke in Yangzhou dialect, and that youth might have sent her to the Mary Magdalene Missionary School for Girls, all the while waiting for her to grow up. When she had finished secondary education and had become a superbly beautiful young woman, Fabio would have gone to her and declared his feelings.

He looked at her now – at that mouth which had been kissed by so many men, and at her beautifully defined chin. Her black cheongsam clung tightly to her figure. She had the body of a woman in a Chinese watercolour painting; a

Westerner needed an understanding of Chinese culture to dream of its soft, subtle curves.

And Fabio did dream. He dreamed that her clothes peeled off to reveal her pearly white skin underneath, skin which was bleached pale because of the late hours she kept. He was filled with confusion. If she were to love him, really and truly, then he would be finished, wouldn't he? Surely he should be grateful that she was only playing with him?

'I'll be off now,' she said, getting up. Her eyes were slightly less red and swollen.

She had shed so many tears for Major Dai, who was no longer on this earth. Fabio was filled with jealousy. If he died, how would she react? She might have a pang of grief, and then she would think: 'Well, he's gone, that man who was neither Chinese nor Westerner. It makes no difference whether he's here or not.' In fact, it made no difference to anyone.

'Have you got all of that, Father?'

Fabio looked at her, puzzled. She tilted her head to one side as if she was going to laugh. Fabio realised she was asking if he remembered everything she had told him about herself. She felt she was someone who, when she had gone, would leave no trace in this world. If Fabio remembered anything at all about her, she wanted it to be that her life had had some meaning.

He felt a pang of pain the like of which he had never felt before.

Sixteen

It was after two in the afternoon when Father Engelmann
returned from the Safety Zone. He had managed to bring
back five or six pounds of rice tucked away in his cassock.
Fabio made rice porridge and called the women and girls
into the refectory. Father Engelmann told them that, just the
day before, the Japanese Army had openly seized scores of
women in the Safety Zone and taken them away. They had
been very devious: first, they had staged the arrest of some
Chinese soldiers; this brought the authorities in the Safety
Zone to the front entrance of the Jin Ling Girls' Academy,
allowing the Japanese to round up the women, take them
out of a side door, and load them onto a lorry concealed

nearby. Conditions in the Safety Zone were worse than at the church, he went on. There was raw sewage everywhere, contagious diseases were rife, and the refugees were fighting over basic necessities. The authorities did not think that a dozen or so thirteen- and fourteen-year-old girls would be any safer there. So Father Engelmann had agreed with Miss Vautrin, the head of the Jin Ling Girls' Academy who was one of the organisers of the Safety Zone, that an ambulance would come to the church that night and take the girls to Dr Robinson's house.

It gets dark early in Nanking in December. By four o'clock it was night. Father Engelmann was taking a nap in his study; he had moved his bed there so as not to have to waste any firewood heating the rectory. It also meant he could hear Fabio Adornato going up and down the stairs and in and out of the building, which he found comforting. In this indirect way, Fabio was company and gave him courage, too.

Fabio raced up the stairs, shouting, 'Father!'

He sounded terrified out of his wits.

Father Engelmann gripped the arms of his chair and tried to raise himself to his feet. His knees buckled and he sat down again. Fabio was at the door.

'There are two trucks outside! I saw them from the church tower!' Fabio shouted.

Father Engelmann stood up. As he did so, the long slash in his goose-down-padded coat gaped open, showing the lining, red like a wound. Fabio looked desperate, as if he had no idea what to do. Neither do I, thought Father Engelmann.

'Go and tell everyone to prepare themselves. Tell them not to make any noise and not to come out under any circumstances.' He put on his black cassock and picked up his crook.

He went into the courtyard, and was greeted by a mass of khaki uniforms; the Japanese soldiers had scaled the wall and were perched on top in serried ranks, looking just like a flock of strange yellow birds blown in on a storm.

The doorbell rang. This time, it was a timid sort of a sound, with a couple of seconds' gap between each ring. Father Engelmann saw Fabio coming out of the kitchen; the women and girls must have received his instructions. He jerked his chin at the younger priest, as if to say: *It's down to you and me now.*

Side by side, they walked to the door and opened the spyhole. This time it was not a bayonet which came through but something bright red. Father Engelmann could see that the Japanese officer was holding up a pot of Christmas poinsettias in his dazzlingly white gloved hand, the petals an intense red.

'What's the point of ringing the bell?' said Father Engelmann. 'I thought you didn't like coming in through the door.'

'Please accept our apologies for the disturbance we caused you last night, Father,' said the officer, clicking his booted heels together and making a deep bow.

He even went to the trouble of delivering this little speech in English.

'Did you really need to bring a group of heavily armed soldiers with you to apologise?' said Father Engelmann.

An interpreter came into view, a cultured-looking gentleman in his fifties wearing gold-rimmed spectacles.

'It's nearly Christmas, and the soldiers have come to bring you Christmas greetings,' explained the interpreter. He seemed to have rehearsed his lines in advance, as his master only smiled without speaking.

'Thank you,' said Father Engelmann perfunctorily, 'and now could you ask your soldiers to get back down off the wall?'

'Father, open the door please.' The request was relayed with unimpeachable courtesy.

'What difference does it make whether I open it or not?'

'You're quite right, Father, it makes no difference at all. So why not show some good manners?' said the interpreter.

Father Engelmann shook his head and led Fabio away.

'Father, it is not wise to offend guests like us,' said the interpreter gently to their retreating backs.

'I used to think that too,' said the priest, looking back at the closed door. 'But then I realised that, whether or not I offend you, it makes no difference to the result.'

'Don't make things worse than they already are,' Fabio muttered.

'Can things get any worse?' said Father Engelmann. There was no way he was going to let these mad dogs in yellow uniforms through the door. To do that would be to elevate them to the status of human beings.

He turned back, to see Japanese soldiers pouring over the wall and into the courtyard. Some of them grabbed an axe and smashed the lock on the entrance door. The officer marched in at the head of another dozen soldiers, who looked as if they were taking over the church.

'Who are you looking for now?' asked Father Engelmann.

There was another bow from the officer. These Japanese certainly were punctiliously polite. 'Father,' the interpreter addressed them ceremoniously, 'please believe that we are making this visit entirely in good faith.' The slightly pained words in English were mimicked by a pained expression on the face of the officer. 'We do so hope that it will make up for any past disagreements between us.'

Father Engelmann gave a very slight smile. There was a glacial look in his deep-set, grey-blue eyes.

'All right. I accept your apology, and your Christmas greetings. Now, let me remind you, that is the exit,' and he turned to show his visitors out.

'Stand still!' shouted the officer. Up till now, he had played dumb and allowed the interpreter to relay his words, but now they burst from him in English.

Father Engelmann stood still but did not turn round. His hunched shoulders expressed resignation.

The officer said something in a fierce undertone to the interpreter, who turned to the priest and said ingratiatingly, 'But we have not started our Christmas celebrations yet!'

Father Engelmann looked at the officer and then around him at the dozens of torches which lit up the courtyard.

Behind the torch beams, the outlines of dark figures could be seen.

The officer spoke again. 'Our HQ wants to hold a Christmas party and I have been ordered to invite a few honoured guests.' He turned to a soldier carrying an attaché case and took from him a large envelope with 'Invitation' handsomely printed on it in Chinese.

'This is very kind of you but I cannot accept any invitation,' responded the priest. He made no move to take the proffered envelope, and it hung awkwardly between them.

'You've misunderstood, Father,' said the officer. 'This invitation is not for you.'

Father Engelmann looked up at the deferentially bowed head of the other. As he grabbed the envelope and opened it, a terrible premonition assailed him. The slight tremor which had started to afflict his hands turned into an uncontrollable shake. The officer told a soldier to shine his torch on the letter. It was addressed to the girls of the church choir.

'We have no choir here,' said Father Engelmann.

'Do not forget, Father, that yesterday you told us there were no Chinese soldiers here either.'

Fabio snatched the invitation from the older priest's hand

and ran his eyes over it. Then, ashen-faced, he turned to the officer. 'Did we not tell you that the St Mary Magdalene schoolgirls had all been taken home by their parents?'

'We have looked into the history of the famous St Mary Magdalene Missionary School. A small number of the girls are orphans.' The interpreter civilly translated the officer's words as if they were all having a perfectly rational discussion.

'They were taken away by the teachers when they left,' said Fabio.

'No. We have accurate intelligence that they have been heard singing hymns. The Japanese Imperial Army has many good friends among the Chinese. Please don't imagine that you can pull the wool over our eyes.'

Father Engelmann was lost in thought, as if the wrangling between Fabio and the officer were of no interest to him and he had more important things to think about. Who had passed on this deadly intelligence? Maybe the informant really believed that the Japanese wanted to repent of their sins, and hear the girls sing hymns. There actually were some Christians, both Protestant and Catholic, among the Japanese troops. Perhaps whoever had betrayed the girls had no idea just how sunk in depravity the Japanese soldiers were. In the

Safety Zone people had talked of how the Japanese soldiers believed that young virgins had restorative powers, and collected their pubic hair which they hung around their neck to ward off evil. They even thought that virgin girls could protect them from a hail of bullets in battle.

Father Engelmann was lost in his musings. Then he pulled himself together to see Fabio bodily trying to block the soldiers' way.

'You have no right to search here!' Fabio shouted. 'If you do, it'll be over my dead body!'

He sounded is if he were ready to be martyred.

Behind the torches there was a slight sound, as a hundred soldiers drew their swords and guns and stood ready for battle.

Father Engelmann sighed. He walked up to the Japanese officer. 'They're only just into their teens,' he said. 'They've led sheltered lives, and they've never had any contact with men, let alone soldiers . . .'

In the darkness, a smile could be seen on the officer's face.

'Please don't worry, Father,' he said. 'On the honour of the Japanese Imperial Army, I promise you that when they have finished singing, I will personally bring them back to the church.'

'Father, how can you possibly believe this nonsense?' said Fabio, lapsing into Yangzhou dialect in his agitation. 'I won't let them do those bestial things!'

'. . . and they cannot accept your invitation,' Father Engelmann went on.

'This will be a very important event for them,' said the officer. 'There will be flowers and good food and music . . . I do not think they would be so foolish as to reject our kindness. That might lead to an unhappy outcome.'

'Officer, this is all too sudden. The children have not had time to prepare themselves. At the very least, they need to have a wash and put on their choir robes. And I need time too, to explain to them what is going to happen and to reassure them there is no need to be afraid. You're the enemy to them. They'll be terrified at the idea of going away with enemy soldiers. In extreme cases, some of them may try to harm or even kill themselves, with terrible consequences.'

Here Father Engelmann gave full rein to his famous eloquence.

'Do you really think these animals want to listen to hymns?' Fabio said to him.

'Father, how long do you think the girls need to get ready?' the officer asked through the interpreter.

'Three hours should be enough.'

'No, no, I can only allow them one hour.'

'Two, at least!'

'No!'

'Two hours is the absolute minimum. You don't want to take a bunch of half-starved, bedraggled, terrified girls with you, do you? Don't you want them to be clean and neat, and willing? I need time to persuade them that you will not harm them.'

His earnestness made the officer pause for a few seconds. 'You can have one hour twenty minutes,' he said finally.

'One hour forty minutes,' pronounced the priest in tones so magisterial they left no room for doubt.

He had won this round.

'Now I want you to take your soldiers out of the church grounds. If the girls were to see you, I could not calm them down and settle their fears. Imagine the sheltered lives they have led. Their school is not much different from a convent. It's been a cradle for their whole lives, they've never left it. So they're exceptionally sensitive, shy and fearful. The sight of occupying forces armed to the teeth before I have properly reassured them might undermine all my efforts.'

The officer barked out a single sentence, which was translated as: 'I cannot agree to that.'

Father Engelmann gave a thin smile. 'Are you really afraid that a small group of young girls will escape your clutches? You have enough troops here to lay siege to a castle.'

This was obviously true and, after a moment's pause, the officer reluctantly gave the order to withdraw from the church compound.

'Father, I can't believe you've been taken in by such nonsense,' said Fabio indignantly.

'I haven't been taken in by a single word of it.'

'Then why didn't you turn down their invitation?'

'Because even if I did, they'd still find the girls.'

'They might not! We could at least try our luck.'

'That's what we're doing. We've gained one hour forty minutes, and we've got to use every minute to think of a way out of this.'

'Think of a way to save your own skin, you mean?' said Fabio rebelliously.

Father Engelmann, far from reacting angrily, appeared not to have heard him. Fabio's English deserted him when he became agitated; his accent and grammar became so hard to understand that Father Engelmann could easily choose not to understand what he was saying.

'We've got a small amount of time. That's better than nothing,' he repeated.

'I'd rather die than hand over those children . . .'

'So would I.'

'Then why didn't you turn them down flat?'

'Well, we can always play for time and then turn them down flat . . . Now, leave me to think.'

Fabio walked towards the library. He looked round and saw the old priest go into the church and sink slowly to his knees before the crucified Christ. While Fabio and the officer were arguing, an idea had flitted across Father Engelmann's mind. Now it was time to pursue that idea, examine it carefully, subject it to dispassionate analysis.

Seventeen

Shujuan and the other girls had overheard Father Engelmann telling the Japanese officer that they needed time to prepare themselves to leave the compound. Their eyes were like saucers. Had the Father lost his mind? They knew that terrible things were happening to women and girls outside the walls of the compound, and so did he. Did he want the Japanese to do the same terrible things to them? The vagueness of their ideas about what these terrible things might be only served to sharpen their terror.

'Maybe the Japanese really will bring us back again,' said one girl.

No one paid any attention to her. The fool was in the

year below Shujuan and had come from the countryside near Anqing.

'Didn't you hear? There'll be good food and flowers –' the girl persisted.

'Then *you* go!' said Sophie, making these apparently inoffensive words sound thoroughly insulting. '*You* go!' she shrieked. Here was a scapegoat on whom she could vent all her despair at the horrors that awaited them. 'The Japanese have lovely food, lovely drink and lovely beds!'

The girl launched herself at Sophie in the gloom and punched her. It did not hurt. In fact, Sophie was grateful for the excuse to lash out at her victim with fists, nails and feet. The girl burst into tears. Then Sophie burst into tears. The other girls sobbed too, as they tried to pull the pair apart.

'You bitch! You smelly bitch!' Sophie shouted, punching and kicking. She did not care now whom she hit. Her need to vent her feelings was overwhelming, and that included her resentment against Xiaoyu. Xiaoyu had gone back on her word and played a cruel trick on her infatuated friend, at a moment when it was a matter of life and death. 'Stinking bitch!' The Anqing girl was a convenient punchbag, and blows and insults rained down on her.

'Who are you swearing at?' The curtain was pulled back and Hongling appeared, followed by Nani and Jade.

'Let's have no more calling people "bitches",' said Hongling. 'A bitch is still a human being.'

'You were such well-spoken girls. Where did you learn such dreadful language?' asked Jade.

'Did you learn it from us?' asked Nani. 'You shouldn't go learning things from people like us!'

The scuffling stopped and the girls quieted down, wiped away their tears and smoothed their clothes and hair.

Only the little girl from Anqing still sobbed.

The curtain parted again and Yumo came out and stood, looking formidable, her arms akimbo.

'What's up with you then?' she enquired in a rich Nanking street slang. 'You can cry all you like, your mum and dad won't hear, but the Japs will.' She jerked a thumb at Hongling, Nani and Jade. 'And less chat from you too.'

After a stern stare, she returned to the women's side, wrenching the curtain back into place behind her.

The girls were startled into silence. Yumo's words sounded so ordinary, like a young mother whose children were getting on her nerves, or a class monitor overseeing a bunch of mouthy younger girls who were supposed to be tidying their rooms. It was just what the girls needed, a casual, rough-tongued scolding, which returned everything to normal.

* * *

Before the crucifix, Father Engelmann got to his feet. Suddenly all thoughts and feelings faded from his mind and he was overwhelmed with exhaustion. Fatigue, hunger and despair had sapped his energy to such an extent that he might not have the reserves of strength to say and do what he had to. He was going to have to be cruel and sacrifice some lives in order to preserve others. They had to be sacrificed because they were not pure enough, because they were second-rate lives, because they were not worthy of his protection, of the church's protection or of God's.

But did he have the right to play God, and make these life-and-death choices? To separate the wheat from the chaff, good from evil, in God's stead? He crossed the courtyard in the direction of the kitchen.

'My children . . .' he would begin, just as he had addressed the schoolgirls countless times before. After all, the others were 'his children' too, weren't they? It struck him as strange that the words did not feel forced, and came easily to his lips. When had it happened, that change in attitude to them? He still did not respect them but his revulsion had gone.

He would put it like this: 'My children, sacrificing oneself for others takes you to a very sacred place. Through sacrificing yourselves, you will become pure and holy women.' But even before he went into the kitchen, he realised that these words were utterly ridiculous, totally false, embarrassing even to himself.

So what should he say?

He almost hoped they would rebel, turn against him, begin to shout abuse. That would give him the strength to say: 'I'm very sorry but you must go with the Japanese. Leave this church immediately.'

There was not a second to waste, yet Father Engelmann still dithered, overwhelmed by indecision.

'Father!' Fabio came running round from the back of the church. 'The graveyard is full of Japanese soldiers. They came in over the wall and they're hiding among the graves!'

Father Engelmann pushed open the kitchen door. There was only one thought in his head: Please let these women be good Chinese women and meekly accept their fate.

Then he stood rooted to the spot.

The women were sitting around the large chopping board, in the middle of which was a guttering candle, looking as if they were holding some sort of secret meeting.

'What are you doing here?' asked Fabio in a low voice.

'I brought them up here,' said Yumo.

'About a dozen of the Japanese soldiers didn't leave with their officers. They've taken over the graveyard!' said Fabio.

Yumo glanced at him, unconcerned. Then she turned to Father Engelmann.

'We have all discussed it –'

'I don't remember you discussing it with us!' exclaimed Jade.

'We'll go with the Japanese,' Yumo went on. 'The school-girls will stay behind.'

For a moment Father Engelmann was stunned. Then he realised what Yumo had said and felt relief wash over him, then guilt at his relief. He hated this ruthlessness in himself.

'You don't really think you'll get wine to drink and meat to eat?' interrupted Fabio urgently.

'Even if there was, I wouldn't go!' said Nani.

'I'm not forcing you,' said Yumo. 'But I can only take the place of one.'

Hongling got lazily to her feet. 'Do you think you're

nobler than Yumo?' She looked at them all. 'Your lives are muckier than pond sludge, and you're all playing Little Miss Precious!' She walked up to Yumo and put her arm around her waist. 'I'm getting into your good books. I'm going with you.'

'Mucky or precious, I've still got my life!' Jade shouted.

'We've still got parents and brothers and sisters to keep on our wages,' some of the others chimed in.

'I haven't put my name down for this. What would I want to go for?'

'Fine!' said Yumo angrily. 'You want to carry on hiding here, cadging off these people? You want to watch the Japs carrying those children off to their doom? You do that! Just who do you think you're saving yourselves for? Is there anyone who gives a toss whether you live or you die?' She was beginning to sound like a foul-mouthed countrywoman, every sentence a stream of curses. 'You think you can hide yourselves away and you'll be reborn as nice young school-girls, just like that? Face it, you were born to be whores, the scum of the earth! But if you do a good deed now, maybe you'll have better karma in the next life.'

Father Engelmann did not really follow what Yumo was saying. It was not just the words she used, but the meaning behind them. But Fabio understood. He had grown up in the countryside where life for women was harsh. It was common to hear them take any opportunity, including scolding their children, to bemoan the sadness of their lives. But so long as they felt that this was their karma, they would always, in the end, accept any injustice fatalistically. Yumo was talking to the women now in terms which they understood. They quieted down.

Suddenly Fabio could bear it no more. 'You don't have to take the schoolgirls' places,' he shouted.

Yumo was taken aback. Fabio felt Father Engelmann's eyes boring into him as he repeated, 'No one need go.'

'Talk sense, Fabio!' said Father Engelmann in English.

'Keep them all hidden in the cellar. Maybe the Japanese won't find them,' said Fabio.

'But the Japanese already know there are schoolgirls in hiding here –'

'That was because you admitted it! You'd already decided to sacrifice these women.' Fabio was so outraged he was scarcely comprehensible and, seeing the older priest was straining to understand, he repeated the accusation. For the first time in his life, he felt Chinese through and through. There was something almost feudal about this xenophobic desire to protect 'his' womenfolk from being ill-treated by any foreign man.

'Fabio Adornato, I'm not discussing this with you.' Father Engelmann's quiet voice quelled the younger man.

There was a ring at the doorbell and the candle flame flickered.

'Get down to the cellar,' Fabio ordered the women. 'You're not going to be dragged off like scapegoats, not while I'm alive to stop it.'

'We're not being dragged, we're volunteering,' said Yumo looking at Fabio. It was a look Fabio had been waiting for, a look that instantly bewitched him. And now the eyes which gave him that look would depart with her body . . .

'I'll go and talk to their officer and ask for another ten minutes,' said Father Engelmann.

'Twenty minutes. It'll take at least twenty minutes for us to put on their clothes,' said Yumo.

It was a clever idea. Father Engelmann was taken aback by Yumo's intelligence and maturity.

'Do you think you can look convincing?' he asked.

Hongling spoke up. 'Don't worry, Father. We can pass ourselves off as anyone except for ourselves!'

'Get the girls' clothes, Fabio, please,' said Yumo. 'Not

the stuff they wear every day. We want what they wear for special occasions, quickly!'

Fabio sprinted to the workshop. Halfway up the ladder it suddenly struck him that Yumo had called him not 'Deacon' or 'Father' but 'Fabio'. And she had made 'Fabio' sound like an authentic Chinese name.

*   *   *

The officer agreed to Father Engelmann's request and his troops waited silently in the chilly night for another twenty minutes. Father Engelmann had explained why they required more time: the choir robes had not been worn for a while. Some needed buttons sewed on, others mending and ironing. The soldiers stood patiently in rows outside the church compound wall, bayonets at the ready. Good things were worth waiting for, and the Japanese were sticklers for ceremony.

Exactly twenty minutes later, the kitchen door opened and out came a group of young girls dressed in wide-sleeved black choir robes. They walked with their heads slightly bent, like girls trying to hide their budding breasts. Each girl carried a hymn book tucked under her arm.

Father Engelmann stood at the gate, making the sign of the cross over each of the women as they passed. It was difficult to tell which of the black-robed women was which. But he recognised Yumo from her height. She brought up the rear of the procession. When she reached him, she smiled shyly and performed a genuflection like a good Catholic schoolgirl.

'You came here seeking protection,' said the priest softly.

'And thank you for taking us in, Father. If you had not, I don't know what terrible things would have happened to us by now.'

Fabio had moved closer and was staring at Yumo.

'Women like us can never escape ruin, or from ruining others,' she added with a sly glance at the two clergymen.

Fabio pulled the heavy door open for the women to pass through. Outside, the torches illuminated a forest of bayonets. The Japanese officer stood to attention, his face in darkness, only the brightness of his eyes and teeth betraying a wolfish delight.

Fabio had never imagined that he would open the door and send these women on their last journey; send this woman, Yumo, on her last journey. Even though Yumo had been born luckless, he had assumed that there was still some shred of hope for her. But not any more. He felt a surge of melancholy. He had first been infected by such feelings as a child when his Chinese adoptive mother took him to operas. She had sown so many seeds of melancholy in his heart. Yes, he thought, seeds grew, and could turn into something quite different.

Beside the burned-out tree, a truck was parked. Two soldiers stood by the tailgate and, as the first 'schoolgirl' approached, they each took hold of an arm and hoisted her up the step. It was no use refusing their help. They blocked any attempt to struggle with drawn bayonets.

Father Engelmann stood at the entrance to the compound. He watched as each woman stepped up and disappeared under the tarpaulin covering. He regretted that he had not asked them their real names, the ones their parents had given them. Eventually all the women were in the truck apart from Yumo. He saw the officer reach out to help her up, and he saw Yumo instinctively jerk away, then give the officer a faint smile. It was the genuine smile of a young girl, shy and modest. She could fool anyone with that smile.

The officer mounted his horse and ordered the truck to start.

'Please wait!'

Father Engelmann ran towards the truck.

The officer on horseback turned to him.

'I'll go with my students,' the priest said.

'*Ii-e!*' the officer replied.

Fabio didn't need to speak Japanese to understand that this meant 'no'.

'I'll go and make sure they sing properly. It has been ages since they last sang . . .' Father Engelmann insisted, trying to climb into the truck.

The officer shouted an order for the truck to pull out. It lurched forward. With a hand clutching the wooden rail of the truck bed and a foot on the rear wheel, the priest was left suspended, his long, black cassock entangling his limbs.

'Father Engelmann!' Fabio called out.

The officer yelled something.

Yumo reached out her hand and placed it on Father Engelmann's.

'Father, you shouldn't . . .'

'Give me a hand, my child . . .' the priest cried out.

All of a sudden the truck picked up speed. Rifles sounded. Yumo screamed as Father Engelmann fell off the truck.

Fabio saw her clutching her bleeding forearm as the priest thudded to the ground. He rushed to his side and called his name, but Father Engelmann could no longer hear.

Epilogue

Shujuan would never forget those last, awful hours in the compound of St Mary Magdalene. No one could speak to or look at anyone else. Fabio gave the girls a hasty dinner of potato soup and then hurried off to the Safety Zone.

The girls sat in the cellar in silence. 'Let us fill our bellies, don't let those prostitutes take our food away,' was the prayer they had been muttering for days. Now they had finally got what they wanted. They had never expected, however, that their prayer would be answered in such a cruel way. As she ate her soup, Shujuan glanced surreptitiously at Sophie, who sat opposite her. Sophie's face was covered in long scratches made by the other girl's nails during the scrum. The marks were the only signs of life on her otherwise subdued face. No one said with regretful sighs: 'Those women saved our lives!' or 'I wonder if they'll survive . . .' But Shujuan knew that all of them, like her, felt pangs of remorse.

When Fabio arrived back, after midnight, it was with a tall Western woman. The girls recognised her as Miss Vautrin. She had brought a barber with her and he shaved the girls' heads. Two hours later, the little band of schoolgirls had been transformed into a band of schoolboys. Miss Vautrin had come in an ambulance and, just before dawn, the ambulance drove away from the church full of sickly young patients, wan and dull-eyed, each one dressed in striped hospital pyjamas which flapped so loosely on their skinny frames that it looked as if there was nothing underneath.

The 'boy' patients spent two days hidden in the sickroom at the Jin Ling Medical Institute. Then they were smuggled out to a place in the nearby countryside, from where they were put onto a boat downriver to Wuhu and then onto another boat to Hankou. Fabio escorted them all the way, in the guise of their doctor.

*   *   *

In the years that followed, China underwent many changes, but Shujuan never changed as much as she did in those few days in December 1937.

Finally reunited with her family, she learned the agony her parents had gone through when they heard the news from China. The moment her father came back from the college where he worked he would sit hunched silently over the wireless, desperate to find out what was happening. There were no telephone and cable links to Nanking. Her father had managed to contact someone in the Chinese consulate, but the answer he got was confused. The situation in Nanking was catastrophic but not a single fact could be verified. He then managed to get through to a friend in Shanghai on the telephone, to be told that some rumours had filtered through to the concessions there: the Japanese Army had carried out a massacre, and some photographs of civilians who had been gunned down had been brought out of Nanking by journalists. As Shujuan lay huddled next to her sobbing friend, imagining her parents enjoying bacon and eggs, they were in fact consumed with anguished remorse, and trying to get boat tickets back to China. They believed, as the Chinese do, that 'if one in the family was to die, then they should all perish together'.

Shujuan kept in touch with Deacon Fabio Adornato. Like her, he had been profoundly changed by his experiences. He left the Church and began to teach world history and the history of religion. He spoke often of Father Engelmann and the inspiration the priest had been to him. Both he and Shujuan shared the faint hope that they might track down one or two of the women who had so bravely gone with the soldiers. At the very least, if they could find out what had happened to them, it would set their minds at rest.

Shujuan was in her twenties when the Japanese War Crimes Tribunal was held in Nanking in 1946. The entire population of Nanking braved the stifling August heat, and descended on the courtroom to witness the public disgrace of the people who had brutally mistreated them for eight years. Milling crowds packed the courtroom; those who could not get in stood in the surrounding streets. Shujuan was outside, one of the crowd listening through the loudspeakers which were strung from telegraph poles. Suddenly she heard a voice she recognised. A woman was in the witness box testifying to the mass rapes planned and carried out by the Japanese military top brass. Although she was using a different name, Shujuan was sure it was Yumo.

It took Shujuan an hour to push her way through the

crowd and get into the courtroom. Once inside, she recognised the woman immediately, even though her back was turned. From behind, she looked as beautiful as ever, in spite of all she had endured. Shujuan squeezed her way through from the edge of the throng, getting soaked in other people's sweat as she did so, and came up behind the woman who had possessed the most famously elegant shoulders in 1930s Nanking. She reached out and tapped one of those shoulders. But the face which turned to hers was not as Shujuan remembered it. Something looked wrong. It was as if, Shujuan felt afterwards, its natural beauty had been destroyed and then clumsily reconstructed by a plastic surgeon.

'Zhao Yumo!' exclaimed Shujuan in low tones. But the woman peered at her in apparent confusion. 'I'm Meng Shujuan!' Shujuan went on.

The woman shook her head. 'You've got the wrong person.' Yet the voice was Zhao Yumo's, the same slightly off-key voice which had so captivated the Nanking playboys of the 1930s when she sang.

Shujuan did not give up. She pushed her way to her side and said, 'I was one of the group of schoolgirls you and the other sisters saved!'

But it was no good. Zhao Yumo kept denying she knew

her. Yet she gave Shujuan a sidelong glance just as Zhao Yumo used to, elegantly lifting the chin which had survived the ravages done to the rest of her face, and spoke in Zhao Yumo's Suzhou-accented Nanking dialect. 'Who is Zhao Yumo?' she asked.

Then she stood up, edged along the rows of seats past people's knees, and left. No one grumbled. How could they when that beautiful chin expressed such exquisite regret at the inconvenience she was causing?

It was, of course, impossible for Shujuan to follow her. No one was going to make way for *her*. She had no option but to go back the way she had come in. By the time she got outside, there was no sign of Zhao Yumo.

She wrote to Fabio Adornato, who was then in America, and told him that Zhao Yumo was still alive. Fabio's grandmother had died in October 1945, leaving her house to him, and Fabio had gone back to sell it. Shujuan told him in her letter how the woman had denied that she was Zhao Yumo. In his reply, which arrived a month later, he said that perhaps it was only by changing her identity that she could go on living. He urged Shujuan to try to put the past behind her now and get on with her life.

Ever headstrong, Shujuan resolved never to give up her

search for the stories of the Qin Huai women. If she didn't remember them, who would? Some information came to her from Japanese journalists' notes and some she got by chatting to Japanese veteran soldiers. But most was elicited from the Chinese she met as she travelled through the provinces of Jiangsu, Anhui and Zhejiang, which surround Nanking.

When Zhao Yumo had given her testimony to the War Crimes Tribunal, she had talked about how, when they were first taken, two of the women had tried to resist with knives taken from the St Mary Magdalene kitchen. They were killed on the spot. The other eleven, when the officers had had enough of them, were deposited in a newly established comfort station. Over the next couple of years, they died one by one; some were executed for trying to escape, others died from disease, and a few even committed suicide. The fact that Zhao Yumo was fortunate enough to survive was probably down to her looks and her style, which meant that she was used by middle-ranking and junior officers. They gradually relaxed their vigilance and eventually she made her escape. That was after about four years of being a 'comfort woman'.

It was only many years later that Shujuan found out what had happened to Cardamom. In an archive she came across a photograph that had been recovered after the war in the notebook of a Japanese POW. In it, a girl was bound to an old-fashioned wooden chair, her legs forced apart and her private parts exposed to the camera lens. The girl's face was out of focus, probably because she was struggling so hard and would not keep still, but Shujuan was convinced it was Cardamom. The Japanese soldiers had not only violated her and condemned her to a lingering death, they had immortalised her humiliation in a picture. The notebook also contained a description of what had happened.

Shujuan closed her eyes and tried to imagine the last moments of the girl who had been barely older than she was. Out in the streets at dawn, alone and drunk, Cardamom would have had difficulty getting her bearings. She had been shut up in the brothel since early childhood, no better than a slave. It was even harder for her to find her way now that the invasion had ravaged Nanking, leaving its houses in ruins or burned out, its streets blocked with overturned carts and the shops emptied of people and goods. She must have wandered about, increasingly confused. Then the Japanese soldiers came.

Shujuan knew what happened next from the soldier's account. They chased after her but Cardamom threw off her pursuers by slipping down a narrow alleyway. That was when she stumbled over a mound of something soft, the spilled entrails of a dead woman. With a shriek of horror, she stood frozen to the spot, trying to shake the ice-cold sticky mess from her hands. It was her undoing. The soldiers had given up the chase but now they were on her. They were joined by a platoon of cavalry camped nearby who had been alerted by the girl's cries.

In a looted shop, a large crowd of Japanese soldiers formed an orderly queue in front of a heavy old wooden chair which they were using as an instrument of torture. Cardamom was tied to it and the soldiers, wearing only loincloths, waited their turn to enjoy her. Cardamom's arms and legs were bound to the chair rests, her legs stretched wide. She swore and spat until the Japanese boxed her ears to shut her up. Then she quieted down, not because she was ready to capitulate but because she suddenly thought of Wang Pusheng. Only the night before she had promised to spend the rest of her life with him. As soon as she finally had four strings for her *pipa*, she had whispered to him, she would play him sonatas, like 'River on a Spring Night' and 'Three Variations on Plum Blossom Melodies'. 'I can sing you Suzhou folk tunes too,' she had told him. But now she never would.

Shujuan remembered listening to Cardamom playing 'Picking Tea' on her one-stringed *pipa*. At the time it had sounded to her like a dirge. Now she thought of it as the most beautiful music she had ever heard.